The Furnace

by
Rose Macaulay

The Furnace
by Rose Macaulay

Copyright © 2024

All Rights reserved.

No part of this publication may be reproduced, stored in a retrieval system, or transmitted in any form or by any means, electronic, mechanical, photocopying or Otherwise, without the written permission of the publisher.
The author/editor asserts the moral right to be identified as the author/editor of this work.

ISBN: 978-93-62203-99-1

Published by

DOUBLE 9 BOOKS
2/13-B, Ansari Road
Daryaganj, New Delhi – 110002
info@double9books.com
www.double9books.com
Tel. 011-40042856

This book is under public domain

ABOUT THE AUTHOR

Dame Emilie Rose Macaulay, DBE was an English author who was born on August 1, 1881, and died on October 30, 1958. She was best known for her award-winning book The Towers of Trebizond, which is about a small group of Anglo-Catholics who cross Turkey by camel. People see the story as a spiritual autobiography because it shows how her views changed and sometimes clashed. Virginia Woolf had an effect on some of Macaulay's stories. She also wrote biographies, travel books, and poetry. Macaulay was born in Rugby, Warwickshire. Her father was a classical scholar named George Campbell Macaulay, and his wife was a woman named Grace Mary Coughlin. Her father came straight from the Macaulay family of Lewis through the male line. After going to Oxford High School for Girls, she went to Somerville College at Oxford University to study Modern History. After leaving Somerville, Macaulay started writing her first book, Abbots Verney, which came out in 1906. She did this while living with her parents at Ty Isaf, near Aberystwyth in Wales. The Lee Shore (1912), Potterism (1920), Dangerous Ages (1921), Told by an Idiot (1923), And No Man's Wit (1940), The World My Wilderness (1950), and The Towers of Trebizond (1956) are some of his later books.

CONTENTS

CHAPTER I
YOUTH IN THE CITY 7

CHAPTER II
THE IMPRESSION-SEEKER 15

CHAPTER III
OF MENTAL STANDPOINTS 21

CHAPTER IV
BLIND WALLS 29

CHAPTER V
BAIÆ'S BAY 38

CHAPTER VI
GRADONI 46

CHAPTER VII
RETROSPECT WITH THE SEARCH-LIGHT 54

CHAPTER VIII
BROKEN BARRIERS 63

CHAPTER IX
FURNACE FLAMES 71

CHAPTER X
BETTY AND TOMMY 77

CHAPTER XI
THE ETERNAL ROADS 85

CHAPTER XII
THE ROADS DIVIDE 95

CHAPTER XIII
PINE-BARK BOATS 102

CHAPTER I
YOUTH IN THE CITY

'Val più aver amici in piazza
Che denari nella cassa.'

Proverb.

Royalty was arriving in the harbour in a steam-yacht. It had, that is, already arrived in the harbour; it was now disembarking on the pier. It was an interesting event. An edified crowd watched it; representatives of the Press jotted down their impressions; some took photographs. A few drew pictures instead. The representative of the *Marchese Peppino*, an illustrated paper widely perused in certain circles, drew pictures; one might gather that it was his intention to be funny, later, when he had leisure to amplify. *Marchese Peppino* always had that intention, and its readers, whose judgment of humour was possibly, however, not of the most delicate or polished type, considered that it usually fulfilled it. The drawings now in process of production were, before they were amplified at leisure, really quite like life; later they would become less so, but no doubt more entertaining. They seemed to be a little funny even now. A man looking over the artist's shoulder giggled and dug him in the ribs. The artist was a nonchalant young man, who did not seem to be amusing himself particularly, but to be working in a wholly professional and business-like spirit. He had quick eyes and clever fingers, and presumably, since he did his job really well, a suitably developed sense of the ludicrous.

Royalty left the pier. It was, presumably, going to have lunch before it admired Naples. That was certainly as well; it gave the representatives of the Press a respite, during which they, too, if they had the inclination and the wherewithal, might have lunch.

The representative of the *Marchese Peppino* sat down on an inverted basket and continued to record impressions, while the crowd thinned slowly.

A facetious young man, passing the artist, made a show of being doubled up with helpless laughter—a mirth presumably anticipatory in nature and complimentary of intent. When he wearied of the compliment he clapped the journalist on the shoulder and observed:

'We shall split our sides on Thursday, ne?'

He cherished an immense admiration for the pictorial staff of the *Marchese Peppino*. The staff gave him his usual melancholy look from under quick brows, and said:

'Have you seen my sister?'

'Just now, talking over there with La Corrini.'

From the group indicated by the jerked thumb the staff's sister emerged. She strolled up to her brother. There did not seem to be any particular difference between them, externally. The boy might have been twenty-three and the girl twenty-two; or it was quite equally likely to be the other way about. At first glance there seemed to be a certain resemblance between them in dress as well as in face; analysis, however, reduced this to the suggestion in each of an untidiness—one might all but say a disreputability—that made their worldly status a matter for speculation. The girl's hat was of broken straw, pulled over her eyes; one of her shoes lacked a lace; her blue cotton dress was sun-bleached and discoloured. The boy wore a ragged blazer, frayed flannel trousers, and a very limp Panama hat, which he kept turning up, with sweet-tempered patience, when it flopped over his eyes.

The girl sat down beside her brother. She had—they both had—a serene air of being admirably content to do nothing during prolonged periods. To sit by the harbour and talk, if the day were fine and the company agreeable, was an excellent afternoon's occupation. The streets were always entertaining, and the harbour particularly so, with the thronging of those who go down to the sea in ships, and the gay greetings of friends, and the cheerful shouting of mariners. Neapolitan loafers (and really to loaf, in the highest sense of that agreeable word, one should go to Naples) always like the harbour. The smell of the sea, too, is pleasant on a hot September afternoon, especially to the unfastidious, who do not cavil at its dilution with various other odours.

The talk between the brother and sister and the cheerful youth who was giving himself a holiday from his shop was leisurely, of an easy familiarity, seasoned with allusions and anecdotes that showed them to share in common a 'set.' The girl's talk was partly professional, of the music-hall stage, on which she made casual and irregular appearances. La Corrini had been saying something to her.... In the report this was very funny. The stout youth, whose name, one gathered, was Luli, roared with laughter and spat many times. It was noticeable that the drawer of pictures, though he, too, talked a great deal, did not spit at all: he only stammered.

Presently they decided to have lunch, and went off, the three of them together, Luli affectionately clinging to the journalist's arm. They turned into a *trattoria* in the Toledo. At one of the marble-topped and not very elaborately cleaned tables a finely developed young woman ate *spaghetti* with admirable speed and dexterity, and drank red Posilipo. The three, seeing her, hailed her with some effusion, and joined her at her table. There ensued a very sociable and conversational repast, and there was a great deal of noise, with the full-bodied and rather strident tones of the young woman of the *spaghetti*, the resonant laughter of Luli, and the stuttering, melancholy-toned and unceasing flow of singularly futile and inane babbling that emanated from the journalist and his sister. These two appeared to have a somewhat extensive circle in Naples; they exchanged greetings with most of their fellow-eaters. Some of these were really comparatively reputable; quite a number were very gaily attired, and most seemed light of heart.

The journalist, after finishing his wine and his inexpensive cigar, announced himself obliged to depart in pursuit of business.

'I must catch them driving out. They are sure to drive out, you know.'

His sister said she too would come, and catch them driving out.

So they went out into the street and sauntered leisurely along it. Its screaming, gay business was a little hushed at this hour of the hot September day; behind closed green shutters people shunned the vertically striking sun; the heavy noon brooded over what was almost, for Naples, stillness. It was not, had the representative of *Marchese Peppino* considered the question, in the least likely that he would at this hour 'catch them driving out.' He very likely did not particularly care whether he so caught them or not; he liked to walk about the streets; neither he nor his sister minded the glare and the hot, baked smell that beat up into their faces. They had an air of very leisurely sweet temper and content with life as it was lived as they sauntered along the Toledo together. There were two things it was manifest that they would not in any circumstances do: they would quarrel with no one, and they would take no thought for the morrow.

'I wonder,' the journalist was saying, 'if Luli would lend us twenty francs. Think he would, Betty?'

He spoke in English now; they always spoke English to each other when they were alone together, though they seemed quite equally at their ease in both languages; they also stammered equally in both. They stammered when they were at all excited, or earnest, or tired, and very often when they were not. When they were talking, these hiatuses were often the only opportunities their companions had of getting in a word edgeways.

Betty thought it improbable that Luli would lend any such sum.

'You know, Tommy, we had ten from him last month. He won't miss it if we don't remind him, but it would be silly to bother him again just yet.'

'Oh, all right. But I'm afraid we've rather got to get some somehow. We've spent an awful lot lately. Why did we have lunch to-day? We didn't want it.'

'Who's been bothering?'

From long experience Betty caught the issue.

'The chap I get paints from. I—I told him he'd got to wait; he c-cut up rough; said he'd waited long enough.'

The stutter, becoming pronounced, showed Tommy a little stirred.

'Well——' Betty's tone was depressed. There was an intonation of melancholy, however, in general in the Crevequers' stammering speech—a melancholy that was on the borderland of laughter, and stuttered into it as a man stumbles unawares into puddles, walking along a wet path. Miss Crevequer, quite suddenly, stumbled into one now, for no apparent reason, and dragged Tommy after her. 'Well'—Betty regained, as it were, dry ground—'let's give him this week's rent; and by next week something will have turned up. You can win some at cards, can't you? It's a pity I've got no job just now. At least, it's rather fun really, and we'll go to the theatre to-night.'

Tommy nodded. The proposition seemed a matter of course; no incongruity struck either. There was, in fact, no incongruity; it was very simple: the payment of debts would have been an indulgence quite beyond their means; going to the theatre was one within them. The Crevequers could only afford cheap pleasures.

They settled themselves for the afternoon under an awning outside a café by which royalty, it was supposed, would eventually pass. There they conversed with friends, and Tommy drew pictures, and time, as usual, passed agreeably and sociably. At about six o'clock there came by an informant, who remarked that royalty had gone for a drive in the opposite direction. Tommy started in pursuit, and did not join Betty again till it was too late for the theatre. So they asked some friends and had a supper-party at a restaurant instead, because the theatre money must be somehow spent. Its spending, and a good deal more besides, proved beautifully easy. Then they came home through the lit streets; the flare of them and the noise of them and the gay people who lounged and talked in them always made the Crevequers feel cheerily at home, and flowing over with the milk of human kindness.

Beyond the flaring, screaming world there was a soft summer moon, nearly at the full, and spaces of silver light on the land and the dark, still sea. But these children of the gay streets had no concern with the moon; the lamps were for them, and the flare of lights that lit the coster's barrow and the pedlar's awning. They loafed along with the true vagrant's air of irresponsible well-being to their home, which was in a narrow street sloping upwards out of the Toledo—sloping up steeply, and laid out in shallow steps.

The Crevequers lived in a flat at the top of a tall pink house. None of the occupants of the house seemed to have yet retired; most of them were in the street outside. The Crevequers stayed for a little to talk to them, then went in and climbed many flights of dark stone stairs, and came at last into the room where they lived. The room had an inexpensive air. It had, however, no lack of contents, and these were, without exception, in unexpected places; the books, for instance, lay on the floor in a corner—a battered selection from the light literature of two languages. There were papers, half-finished drawings, writing and painting materials, littered over the table among half-emptied bottles, cigarettes, and unwashed glasses. The ceiling was interesting; it was partially covered with a design in bold colours, unfinished; it gave the impression of being worked at, spasmodically, at irregular intervals, by more than one artist; it had an interesting air of awaiting the next inspiration. It was an untrammelled composite, so far, of the beauties of nature, imaginative and highly exciting dramatic incident, and scenes from pagan lore, with, whenever imagination or space required padding, a cherub plunging through a festoon of flowers. Some of the designs bore a vaguely familiar air; the visitor to Pompei might have recognized, for instance, the lady on her knees with a bird's-nest full of infants. The most note-worthy point about this ceiling was that it was really not badly painted.

The most comfortable features of the room were two large arm-chairs, one on each side of the stove. Tommy cleared a space in one of them and subsided into it. Betty dragged a spirit-lamp and a saucepan of milk from under the table and knelt over it, whistling a soft, tired little tune the while. Tommy, lying in his chair, whistled too, feeling in his pockets for matches.

'Cocoa, Tommy?' Betty broke her tune to say.

'No.' He had found a match, and was scraping it perseveringly on his knee. 'It's going to boil over,' he remarked.

She caught it off with a deft hand and poured it into a cup, and, carrying it to the other arm-chair, in which she did not trouble to clear a space, she lay back with a sigh of contented languor.

'Cigarette, please. Thank you.'

There was a battering at the door, and an influx of three youths and two young women. It seemed that they had been having supper together—enough supper to raise their spirits and to make them very sociable and amiable. The Crevequers, having also had supper, were sociable and amiable too, and Tommy got out more wine, and the room became blue with smoke and full of laughter; and Tommy played his banjo, and Betty sang a song which amused them all very much, and the three young men and the two young women shouted the chorus. None of the other occupants of the house seemed to be disturbed—they were probably used to it. The company stayed late. These pleasant gatherings are hard to break up, and the Crevequers' friends seemed attached to them. With the young man who had drunk most wine Tommy made a bet and won it; it was a five-franc note, and it was satisfactory as it changed hands to feel that the loser, in his then state of warm generosity, did not at all miss it. Tommy did a further stroke of business by arranging an evening of cards with this gentleman for the following week. At last, with hilarious leave-taking, the visitors departed, some to their rooms in the same house, some elsewhere, all very merry and affectionate.

'It hasn't been a really busy day—not so very,' Betty remarked presently. 'Why are we tired?'

'There seems to have been plenty to do, one way and another,' Tommy said, still gently fingering the banjo-strings.

They spoke languidly. The tiredness of their faces seemed to slur over the delicate discriminations that really existed between them. They were, as a matter of fact, not quite exactly alike at ordinary times. For example, Betty had a dimple, when she laughed, in her left cheek; Tommy's indentation, rather fainter, was in his right. Both had blue eyes glinting to grey, but the longer sweep of Betty's lashes made hers oftener approach to black. When their eyes flickered from melancholy to sudden laughter, as they did rather often, and usually on quite unexpected and incongruous occasions, they had a trick of narrowing to blue slits. The slant of the black brows of both was up, slightly, from left to right; they were quick brows, that flickered a little with their speech.

'Let's get on our dressing-gowns and brush our hairs,' Betty suggested.

She went into one of the two adjoining rooms, and returned with a red dressing-gown and a hair-brush, and curled herself up in her chair.

'Tommy, you really have done that faun's right leg so very badly—it's getting a bad dream to me.'

physically, intellectually, and spiritually. Quite a pagan, but his wife was a Roman Catholic, and I heard that the children were brought up to her faith, though she died quite young.... One feels always about his books that they should be intensely interesting, but it is an interest somehow run off the lines.... And so that is Maddan Crevequer's boy!'

The thought suddenly brought her up. The flare of a street lamp had shown Tommy Crevequer rather plainly—his bare head, his frayed blazer, his friends, girls and men, who laughed. It was, perhaps, his friends who chiefly put the ring of surprise into Mrs. Venables' tone. Interest followed close on its heels. The thing struck her.

'Curious. We must find him out, Warren; get to know him.'

'Must we, mother? Good copy, do you think? But one knows the sort'—he made a downward movement with his hand—'when it's sober it borrows, and that's such a bore. Besides, we shan't be able to find him—and he won't, probably, want to be found.'

'You might go back now....'

'Interrupt the reading? No, I think not. He mightn't be pleased.'

'He looked,' said Mrs. Venables, 'as if he was entering into the life of the quite poor. That would be an enterprise of immense interest if one could really accomplish it, really break down the barriers. We must find the boy, Warren.'

'All right, we'll try. But I expect he's just scum, you know. There are lots like him in every big town; it drifts about the bottom, that sort, and personally I don't think it's anything in its favour that it's by way of being—or having been—a gentleman. But I've no doubt you'd like it, mother, so we'll look for Crevequer. Only its not an easy sort to find, I warn you. Nomadic, you know.... Oh, of course Crevequer may be just on the spree for to-night; he may dress better as a rule.'

The impression of Mr. Crevequer seemed to remain with Mrs. Venables, standing out above the other dishes of her orgie. She returned to her hotel replete.

Tommy Crevequer met his sister at the door of the Fondo Theatre, and walked home with her. He mentioned Venables.

'Head of my house in my first year at school. He was decent to me, rather. I don't suppose he knew me to-night; he had some one with him, so I didn't stop him; but I wouldn't mind meeting him again.'

It was quite clear that he would not mind in the least. The Crevequers never minded meeting people; they were very sociable.

Betty said that Morello had asked her to sit to him.

'I suppose I'd better—had I? It will bore me quite awfully, but it would be extravagant not to, of course. And he's asked Gina and me to supper to-morrow. You'd better come too; it may be fun.'

Tommy hummed an air.

'He's a silly ass, Morello is. But we'll have supper with him by all means, particularly with him and Gina; Gina's great sport.... It's struck me, Betty, that perhaps Venables did know me, and was feeling proud or something. If he's proud I should love to meet him again, and introduce him to—to Luli and every one. It would be our duty, don't you think? But Venables used to be an awfully good sort—I don't believe he's really proud—and if we do run into him again, we'll take him about with us.... I'm awfully hard up just now.'

The Crevequers did not suffer from pride.

Three weeks later, Venables walked into the Crevequers' room. It was about six o'clock; the Crevequers had guests, who smoked and drank wine and conversed. Tommy Crevequer sat astride on the table; Betty was on the arm of a chair, leaning back against Gina Lunelli's broad shoulder. It was confusing to come into such an intimate party.

Tommy looked round, and broke off in the middle of what he was saying, and got off the table. He was glad Venables had come. Venables apologized.

'How are you, Crevequer?... But I'm interrupting you; I'll come in another time.'

But Tommy drew him in, and introduced him to Betty, and to Luli and Gina and all the rest, and offered him wine. It was a convivial gathering; Venables, being a stranger, and wearing a rather clean collar, perhaps threw a shade of restraint over it, but mirth broke out again before long. At last, with common accord, the company took its leave—all but Venables.

'Well, how are you Crevequer? I've been looking for you, you know, all over the place.'

Tommy had almost forgotten how much he had admired Venables once; it returned to him now as they talked. He would have liked to see a good deal of Venables. Venables painted, he learnt—painted successfully, Tommy presumed, looking at the clean collar and the well-cut coat. It was perhaps a pity, Tommy reflected, his melancholy eyes, under their quick, amused brows, turning from Venables to his sister, that he and Betty were not better dressed to-day. Venables was probably a person of prejudices, and his collar was very clean.

Venables learned that Crevequer was a journalist.

'What's your paper?'

'That.' Tommy indicated *Marchese Peppino* on the table; it came out that day.

'Oh.'

Venables just glanced at it; he showed no desire to inspect it more closely; possibly he knew enough about it already. His clever face was scrupulously devoid of expression.

'I chiefly do sketches,' Tommy elaborated. 'You know the sort of thing? They aren't funny, not a bit; but they sell. Oh, I write for it, too, of course; and that's funnier, rather. *Novelle in corto*, you know; we have the news in, as much as if we were anybody; combine instruction with amusement, don't you know.'

Venables knew quite well.

'I wonder,' he thought afterwards, '*why* he shoved it down my throat like that. Mere cheek, perhaps, or to show he didn't mind, or to warn me off at once in case I didn't like his style. Or doesn't he really, perhaps, realize....'

Not really to realize, Crevequer must have pushed very far from the shores of decency.

Venables let the topic of *Marchese Peppino* lie where Tommy had dropped it. He delivered his mother's message, not stiffly, but with voice and face a little vacant of expression, lacking interest. He asked the Crevequers to come to lunch to-morrow at Parker's Hotel. Mrs. Venables had not been aware of Betty, but Warren supposed that her existence would add a further element of picturesque interest to the 'impression.' The invitation was accepted. Venables stayed a little longer, and examined the ceiling, and discovered incidentally that the Crevequers—probably by the sheer insane futility of their stammering flow—had the power of pricking him at all points to sudden laughter.

He considered it walking home. In his search for Tommy Crevequer he had happened upon a man—he kept a billiard saloon—who knew him rather well. His remarks, entirely friendly (he was really fond of Tommy), conveyed to Venables several items of information about him; among others, that Venables would at no time have any difficulty in finding him, as a good many people thought it prudent to keep him under view. At the same time, Tommy's acquaintances seemed to assume as a matter of course that he might find an occasional plunge into obscurity a convenience. These casually conveyed impressions Venables had assimilated without surprise. As he would have said, one knew the sort. And Venables liked people who amused him.

But *Marchese Peppino* stuck in his throat.

Betty observed to Tommy:

'What fun. We shall probably forget to go. But if we don't, we shall have to eat so much that we shan't need any more for a week. How economical! Lunch in England—do you remember, Tommy?'

Tommy was thinking.

'Betty, we don't dress well enough. I want a new hat; so do you. Venables is better dressed than we are. We must be tidy, and cut a dash at lunch. It's a mistake not to be well dressed; people are so prejudiced. I shall wear a collar to-morrow—a quite clean one, like Venables. And we won't have any supper to-night, because we shall have to eat too much at lunch. And I suppose Mrs. Venables will talk about father's books, as she's so interested; so let's read them.'

'Perhaps,' said Betty, 'we'd better read her own works too; only I don't feel sure they'd be quite nice, so I think we'll wait till we're older—thirty-two and thirty-three. We can tell her if she asks that we read so little that we have to be very careful about what we read. It would be so disappointing to read a book we didn't like; she'll understand that.'

CHAPTER III
OF MENTAL STANDPOINTS

'E parea posta lor diversa legge.'—Dante.

The Crevequers, as they had anticipated, did eat too much at lunch—a good deal too much. They cast, occasionally, wondering and interested glances round the dining-room, and took in the fact that every one at all the little tables was also eating too much. It was borne upon them that this exorbitance, a strange incident in their own lives, was to these others a daily occurrence. Every day at one o'clock the dining-room at Parker's, the dining-rooms at all the hotels of its genus, were filled with Anglo-Saxons and a few others, all sitting round little tables, and all eating too much. Then again at dinner-time.... The impressiveness of the thought widened their eyes, filling them with an awestruck solemnity. To eat too much, a good deal too much, twice—nay, thrice—a day (for visions of the Anglo-Saxon breakfast haunted them: one had honey, one ordered omelette) during a period of weeks and months—it required thinking over quietly afterwards. At present, face to face with the amazing succession of the courses, the contemplation of all it meant made one a little dizzy. The Crevequers took all the courses; they would not have missed one; they intended to see this thing through. As they ate they talked stammeringly. Mrs. Venables was struck by the melancholy of their pondering eyes. Her interest—she had an immense fund of it—was gathering itself together to pour itself unstintedly forth on Maddan Crevequer's children. Her son and her daughter and her niece watched the gathering; it was a familiar process to them. The son watched it with languid amusement; the daughter with stolid unconcern (she was a bored child of eighteen); the niece with eyes inscrutably remote. The Crevequers were copy; they came to be studied, to be drawn out; they responded to the process with their usual affability. They answered questions as to their way of life, their friends, the customs of the Neapolitan poor, their religion. Mrs. Venables, as she said, found the Roman Catholic standpoint quite immensely interesting. The Crevequers groped uncomprehendingly after the reason of such interest, and gave it up. They were, however, quite ready to answer the questions put to them; it seemed a harmless craze enough. Mrs. Venables had been to Mass the day before, and had, she affirmed, been much struck by the impressive contrast of the ordered stateliness of the service and the spontaneous gaiety of the people as they trooped out into the piazza afterwards. It had occurred to her, watching the devout worshippers, that Catholicism was in some of its aspects a strange medium for the spiritual interpretation of the blithe Italian genius. What did Mr. Crevequer think?

Mr. Crevequer thought, but did not say, that she might have been more profitably employed in attending to the service than in watching the devout worshippers.

Mrs. Venables' niece, Prudence Varley, talked about Naples, with a certain careful accentuation of the purely ordinary point of view of the cultivated seer of sights. Her cousin Warren, watching her, smiled inwardly at the accentuation. He understood it perfectly well. There was in it a certain quality of externality that gained edge from the contrast with Mrs. Venables' all-reaching intimacy. It revealed, anyhow, how the Crevequers wallowed in ignorance—how they knew nothing. Museums, mosaics, pictures, sculpture, were to them less than names. Churches they knew only in so far as they went to church in them; and it was not from the point of view of one interested in worship, but in architecture, that Miss Varley seemed to approach the subject, differing herein from her aunt. When she discovered that the Crevequers knew nothing, she did not follow the subject; she gently fell again into her non-conversational attitude, which seemed almost a little abstracted. (She had often that air.) The Crevequers had indeed their own knowledge of Naples—none more so; but it was the intimacy of streets and corners, that close acquaintance with the face of a city which belongs to those who, as Warren Venables had said, 'drift about the bottom.' How should they know of mosaics? They knew every little narrow *gradone*, shut in with leaning houses, that led steeply up out of all the length of the Toledo, from Piazza San Carlo to the doors of the museum. (Beyond the doors their ignorance began.) They knew at what hour on Friday mornings it was most amusing to be playing round Porta Nolana; they knew the price at which you can get a plate of macaroni and a mezzo-litro of wine at all the *trattorie* (of any economy) in Naples, and at which you were most likely to meet amusing acquaintances, and at what hours. But it was possible that Miss Varley felt no more curiosity as to these things than the Crevequers as to the Angevin tombs in Santa Chiara. In Naples there seemed to be no meeting-ground, or none which Miss Varley cared to seek. It was Mrs. Venables who talked of Pompei—of the unique, almost oppressive, so she said, interest of it. The Crevequers knew Pompei as a place with nice hot, bright streets, scampered over by lizards, where it was agreeable to spend an afternoon among the gaily-hued, roofless houses, and go to sleep. But, they said, Christian Pompei was a better place—it had more variety. Here the gulf yawned aggressively; Mrs. Venables strove to throw a bridge by remarking that to some mental standpoints the present teemed with an eternal interest that quite obscured the past. The Crevequers supposed that this might be so.

Young Miranda Venables said that she thought the past was an awful bore. She did not approve of Naples; she was vexed at missing the hockey and beagling season at home, and she thought towns were beastly, especially Italian towns. She hated them. She looked towards the Crevequers with a rising of hope; here, it seemed, were two people who lacked intelligent interest even as she did. Miranda was, from her mother's point of view, a failure. She was in no way æsthetic, except sartorially. The Liberty frocks and flopping hats that her soul loathed seemed to give an edged incongruity to her pleasant round face, with its rosy cheeks and blue eyes, and mouth that drooped pathetically at the corners. She did not rebel against the bitter yoke of the picturesque: it was not worth while; she was merely used to remark, with her customary forcible elegance of phrase, that if her mother chose to spend money on making her look a guy, it was her look out, though Miranda considered it a pity that she could not get better value than that for her outlay. But her soul was not at all in her clothes; it was in quite different things—chiefly in hockey.

She raised that theme.

'I say, couldn't we get up a sort of a club? There must be a ground somewhere.'

But the Crevequers, it seemed, did not play hockey. It was sad how everywhere gulfs yawned. Miranda sighed, and fell back upon her lunch. That remains, even in Naples.

The Crevequers, on their side of the gulf, talked; they were really quite entertaining; their acquaintance included such various types of persons, their experience such interesting incidents. Some of the incidents revealed them, personally, in a light rather unusual—a light not apt, as a rule, to illumine a lunch-party. Of this they were sublimely unconscious; at their ignoring of it Warren Venables smiled a little. They were wholly innocent of the half-humorous, half-boastful posturing of the conscious rake; these things, assumed as the basis of their stories rather than narrated, were to them entirely natural—a matter of course. From the same outer darkness—Venables came to believe it was that—Tommy had discoursed of *Marchese Peppino*. It was not that they considered themselves reputable people, but simply that reputability (and the word includes in this case common honesty) was a thing wholly ignored by them, outside their sphere of knowledge. Certainly, such ignoring obviated embarrassment. Meanwhile, to entertain a tableful of strangers at lunch is an admirable gift. Mrs. Venables, possibly, did not sufficiently appreciate it; being amused came very much lower down on her scale of pleasures than being interested; it was perhaps fortunate, therefore, that it was a pleasure much rarer of attainment. She did not desire it of the Crevequers; she desired, as she phrased it, to draw them out, to achieve a near and serious intimacy.

When every one had finished eating too much (the Crevequers wondered to each other afterwards why it had come to an end just at that point, no sooner and no later; they themselves, once wound up to eat continuously, could have carried it on indefinitely), Mrs. Venables found a divan for herself and Betty in a secluded corner of the large hall, and continued the process of eduction. She had formed a plan; she wished of all things to come into contact with the real life of the people; she wanted Tommy and Betty to help her.

'You must be so delightfully intimate with them. With me they may be suspicious and reserved at first. And I am not at all completely mistress of the language. But I can at all events give them a very genuine sympathy and interest; and it would please me to try the experiment. I know something of our girls in London who work at the great factories. If we could form a sort of club here—social evenings, and so on—your help would be of immense value to me. You have achieved a real intimacy—you and your brother. To share the same faith must be a tremendous bond; there is no more tenacious or more beautiful tie, as Tolstoy says.... You remember the passage, perhaps?'

Betty shook her head.

'We don't read much, Tommy and I don't. There seems always something else to be done, out in the streets or somewhere.'

'The true pagan joy in mere living,' reflected Mrs. Venables, and continued: 'If one could call oneself, definitely, a member of any faith.... But one cannot, after all, sacrifice truth to beauty—even to the beauty of sympathy and close community with others.... You are happy in having found a firm foothold.'

Mrs. Venables was not crude enough to ask questions on these subjects; she drew confidence gently towards her. Doubt found in her always a ready hearer. But Betty, it seemed, was not in doubt.

A further step in intimacy Mrs. Venables achieved.

'If there is anything I can do to help you.... I should be glad, you know, to be of any service to your father's children.... We must see a great deal of each other.'

'Thank you very much,' said Betty, considering.

Mrs. Venables perceived the pondering glance of the melancholy eyes, and leaned forward, laying a gentle hand on the thin childish one, waiting confidence.

'Well ... if you would be so awfully kind as to l-lend us twenty francs,' the sad tones stammered.

'Lend you....'

Mrs. Venables drew back; her surprise startled Betty. It was, surely, a very usual and natural request.

'Of course,' Mrs. Venables said gently, after a moment. 'I will give it to you now.... I am so sorry....'

'Thank you tremendously.'

Betty put the notes in her purse. Mrs. Venables became aware that the Crevequer smile, with the single dimple, was rather engaging. Then Tommy came up with Venables, and said it was time to go away.

Miss Varley, as she said good-bye, referred to Betty's statement that she sometimes posed.

'Will you for me? I am painting a picture, and I should be very grateful if you would.'

The unsmiling directness of the tone made the request very much a matter of business. Betty said she would.

'Warren and Prudence are always painting,' Miranda explained mournfully. 'Their pictures are rotten, I think; I hate them.'

The Crevequers went.

'Very picturesque; very striking; very sad,' Mrs. Venables observed.

'Very obvious,' Warren commented. 'I would have betted a guinea that Crevequer would borrow from me; he did. I call that so obvious as to be tiresome.'

To his cousin, a little later, he remarked:

'You're standing on a quite false pedestal of superiority, you know. Because you're going to paint her yourself. Where's the difference?'

'Ah, well, there is some. To me she's frankly copy, you see; I shall pretend nothing else; I shan't call it making friends—don't you see? There's where it comes in.'

'All the same, you'll be doing what you repudiate; you'll be making use for your own ends of what you wouldn't otherwise have anything to do with. You're in a false position; you can't escape that by sophistries.'

'If I am, I shall have to be more than ever careful not to make it falser by throwing veils over it,' said Prudence Varley consideringly.

She had the air of a person of a very delicate sense of justice—delicate almost to exaggeration. One detected it in her farsighted grey eyes, with the twinkle that lurked just within call.

Warren chuckled.

'Poor model! You needn't make it so hard as all that for her; let her have a veil or two—it's so much more comfortable.'

Prudence shook her head with decision.

'It wouldn't be fair; it would be ugly.'

Warren smiled again—at her characteristic habit of arriving, with great deliberation, at her own position in a matter, and remaining in it unshaken. If to her perception an immense difference stretched between the frankness of taking copy as such, and ending there, and the course of tact and sympathy and 'achievement of intimacy' which his mother pursued, no accusations of sophistry or overniceness would bridge that gulf to her.

'Well,' Venables said, half defensively, 'Mother really is interested, you know—very much so.'

Prudence frowned over it, half abstractedly.

'As I see it, you either like people or you don't. If you don't, and yet make use of them, they've got to know how the thing stands and all about it.'

'The Crevequers, you know,' Venables said, 'are quite clever enough to know "all about it," even if you do use a veil or two.'

'Are they?' Prudence's eyes mused. 'Oh, I dare say they're clever enough to know. But, Warren, I have a feeling about them—it came to me in the middle of lunch, quite suddenly—that they *don't* know; that, somehow, either because they are made so, or because they've missed their chances, they know—well, really very little indeed about themselves and how they stand. And that—if that's so—makes it worse; because, do you see, if we accepted them, they would take it naturally, and be content to be accepted; and all the time there would be all kinds of things between us, that we knew of and that they didn't. That would be ugly. Don't you see? But if we don't accept them, the things between don't matter; it's all right and fair.'

'Well, it may be. Anyhow, if that's what mother would call your "mental standpoint," I'm a little sorry for Miss Crevequer. It will be an embarrassing sitting—except that I can't quite imagine either of you embarrassed.... Personally, you know, they amuse me quite a lot.'

'Oh, well, as to that——' The twinkle came to the front of the grey eyes.

The Crevequers, lounging about Santa Lucia that evening, had their own comments to make. They were a little puzzled.

'Why *not* be a Catholic?' Tommy pondered, with knitted forehead. 'What else should a man be? Why is it funnier than to be a heretic, or a Jew, or a Buddhist? Perhaps those things *are* interesting, though, if once one begins thinking about them. We aren't interested in enough things, Betty. Let's study agnostics, and begin with Mrs. Venables. We'll ask her how she feels in church, and say "this is most impressive," as she does. Do agnostics go to church, at least?'

'She does. She watches the devout worshippers. We must think of some nice striking things to tell her, Tommy. She likes that, and we ought to do it, as they've been so kind to us—about how the contadini round Baja still pray to Pan, and things of that sort, that foreigners always like to hear. Would she take that, do you think? No, not quite, perhaps—rather risky. It was very nice of them to lend us both money; and they won't be in a hurry, I should think. I shall rather like to sit to Miss Varley; she's nice to look at, don't you think? She doesn't say very much, but then I can do that.'

'Well, I call them all rather decent,' Tommy said.

They stood for a little and listened to the soft sound of the little night waves scraping the shingle, and looked over the still, dark bay, cut across by the golden road of the three-quarter moon, to where the pine-shaped column above Vesuvius hung and blazed intermittently.

'Something ominous in that sign that the sleeping monster still lives,' murmured Betty. Then, in answer to a questioning stare, 'Not my own—Mrs. Venables. Tommy, I'm sleepy; let's go to bed.'

'No,' said Tommy—'supper at Brunati's. We'll find some one to have it with us.'

Betty looked dubious.

'To-morrow, don't you think? We really did have such a splendid lunch....'

'To-night,' said Tommy recklessly. 'They must have had tea just after we left them, and dinner after that, and I expect they eat more at it than they did at lunch. We're as good as they are, I should think.'

CHAPTER IV
BLIND WALLS

'The internal nature of each being is surrounded by a circle, not to be surmounted by his fellows; and it is this repulsion which constitutes the misfortune of the condition of life.'—Shelley.

'Our eyes are hidden that we cannot see things that stare us in the face, until the hour arrives when the mind is ripened.'—Emerson.

'Forty-six—ninety-eight—fifteen—sixty-three—twenty-seven,' little Silvio Sardi announced at the door of the Trattoria Buonaventura, at the top of his strident young voice.

When he had repeated it three times, every one understood. The expectant stir gave place, in general, to flat disappointment. It is unfortunate to be so sanguine that the weekly disappointment loses none of its force with repetition.

But Tommy Crevequer stood up suddenly.

'Ninety-eight and sixty-three. I say, Betty——'

Betty nodded.

'They're ours all right. The ambo; that's how much—seventy-five francs.'

The Crevequers were rapid and accurate at mental arithmetic.

Congratulation buzzed round them.

Some one raised a voice of anguish.

'Madre Dio, I should have won the terno if I'd staked the numbers my husband had from the parocco, and I forgot all about it!'

The general opinion, conveyed by shrugs and expressive pursings of the lips, seemed to be that this was a great pity for Maddalena. They all knew her husband, who was a Guardian of the Public Security and a hard man. A friend of his remarked, in a confidential undertone, with no uncertainty on the subject, 'He'll cut her throat for her.'

'It won't be the first time if he does,' returned his neighbour. 'Dio! what a fool!'

A man from a table in a corner got up and came over to the Crevequers, and sat down beside them, with an aspect of resolution, good-humoured but adamant.

'I shall come with you when you fetch it,' he observed, nodding cheerfully.

Tommy looked at him, his eyebrows a little aggrieved.

'Oh, Grollo, you— —I tell you, I've any amount to do with it; it will go no way.'

'On the contrary, it will go nearly all the way. For the remaining five francs I'll wait.'

'I've got to get my evening clothes out of pawn; I'm going out to dinner on Monday.'

'Well, you must go as you are, then.'

Tommy looked at him resentfully.

'Well, half, then—forty?'

'I shall come with you when you fetch it,' the creditor repeated, good-temperedly stubborn.

'Oh, well— —' Tommy shrugged his shoulders resignedly. 'Come, then; I shall fetch it now. Coming, Betty?'

'No.'

Betty was talking to Gina Lunelli. Gina was a fine young woman, rather beautiful, with black curly hair, and an immense amount of experience, on and off the music-hall stage, for her twenty-seven years. She was a great friend of the Crevequers; it rather entertained her that anyone should be so silly and so young. All the men she knew made love to her as a matter of course—or possibly she made love to them; it, anyhow, between the two, was invariably made. Tommy Crevequer's love-making was to both an excellent joke; to Betty also, for they were nearly always a three-cornered party. Gina and Betty went out now and stood in the street and talked; or rather Gina talked, and Betty listened and rather often laughed; it took very little to amuse the Crevequers. Soon Tommy came back; he carried a parcel; his face was rather gloomy.

'Grollo's got it all,' he remarked resentfully. 'But I've got my dress-clothes; I met Venables.'

'He who walks home from the theatre with you?' Gina said to Betty.

'Yes. He's always so kind about lending us money,' Betty explained.

Gina nodded. She had once been introduced to Venables in the Crevequers' room; she had been a little embarrassed with him; it was a type outside her fairly wide sphere of experience.

'Well, good-bye till to-night; I must go.'

The Crevequers walked home through the darkening December afternoon.

'Venables is really decent,' Tommy observed, with some enthusiasm.

Betty nodded. They had seen a good deal of Venables lately. Yesterday he and Betty had been to Baja in a motor-car; it had amused them both very much. He was a good companion, being quite ready and able to enter into the game of being hopelessly silly, which, the Crevequers had long since found, very many people, otherwise pleasant, quite failed to understand. Nobody, it seemed to them, understood it quite as well as they did themselves; it was fortunate, therefore, as they sometimes remarked, that they had each other to go about with.

In the evolution of relations with the Venables, that with Warren seemed now to be, on the whole, the most satisfactory. The relation with Mrs. Venables, though her own 'achievement of intimacy' suffered no flagging, had been to the Crevequers a little spoiled by a renunciation on their side. For sometime they co-operated readily and cheerfully in the process of eduction; knowing it their business to 'strike,' they did their best to do so, laying on effects sometimes a little over lurid. They instituted competitions as to which of them could call forth most often during an interview the comment 'very striking.' Tommy usually won, because, as Betty complained, Mrs. Venables was more easily struck by boys than by girls. It was Tommy who appropriated Betty's idea of the worship of Pan that lingered in country districts about Naples.

'That's why goats are so common, all about the streets—don't you know?'

He turned to Miranda, who nodded.

'I know. Beasts. I hate them.'

Mrs. Venables was stirred.

'So vestiges of paganism really do linger. That is extremely striking.'

Tommy, pluming himself, happened to look across and meet Miss Varley's eyes fastened consideringly upon him. He returned the regard with his melancholy gaze.

'Not only Pan, either—Venus, Jupiter, Mars——'

'Don't!' Miranda interrupted. 'You're going on just like my astronomy mistress. She was a beast. I hated her. And I hate stars. And you do talk rot, you two. You both tell the most awful——'

But Tommy was looking at Miss Varley with his sad regard from under quick black brows.

She turned to her aunt and started a new subject.

Tommy remarked to her as he said good-bye:

'I'm sorry you thought I was so rude.'

She looked at him for a moment.

'I shouldn't have thought you were particularly sorry, you know. Good-bye.'

The leisurely considering tone, that quite lacked interest, seemed to add an edge to the words.

Tommy, going home with Betty, observed:

'I'm not going to be striking any more. Miss Varley looks at me, and it makes me so shy, and when one's shy one isn't convincing.... I suppose it's really rather a rotten game, you know.'

Betty admitted that it might be so. So that renunciation was made, and their relation with Mrs. Venables became less amusing to themselves and, presumably, less edifying to her. It was quite wearying having to be so comparatively literal.

The Crevequers wondered if Miss Varley appreciated the sacrifice. Betty did not imagine her likely to notice it; she was a person of abstraction. She took an interest, it seemed, in nothing but her work. To be in her presence—in her studio, for instance—was a little like being in the cold, rarefied atmosphere of a mountain-top. It was curious, always, to plunge suddenly into it. To get back afterwards into the warm valleys was also rather curious. Her conversation, when she had any, was a little obvious in its conventionality. It seemed to Betty, when she looked at her, surprising that this should be so. She was pleasant to look at, slim and tall, with head poised a little high, a little backwards; her short upper lip was caught up a little from her lower, seeming to carry out the character of the round, lifted chin and backward-poised head. Over her far-seeing grey eyes her fair brows often puckered thoughtfully, as if they strove to discern. The winter sunshine, striking in through the window, made of her light hair a fluffy aureole. There was, perhaps, a Puritan touch somewhere about her, emphasized by the simple lines of her green painting-smock. There was also something remote, inaccessible. Her grey eyes, dwelling on Betty, were artist's eyes; they seemed to take in every line, carefully noting, and to give out nothing. There was in their regard a certain quality of reserve, an implication of something held back.

Betty, returning the look with her own melancholy child's gaze, took it in without interpretation or analysis. It happens sometimes that for the interpretation of a look we have to wait for spaces of years. Apprehension is a thing of gradual growth; sudden lightening is rare.

Betty felt it a pity that Miss Varley was not a more conversational person, or at least that her conversation should be so very unexciting, so obvious. In the unquiet condition of Vesuvius, in the fact that a great number of visitors were staying in Naples, Betty felt not the least interest. But Miss Varley seemed disinclined to talk of other things; when the conversation tended to become at all autobiographical she became inattentive and absorbed. Betty, lest she should become bored (an unthinkable calamity), started a game, something of the nature of that which she and Tommy played with Mrs. Venables; the object in this case was to produce the sudden curve of the lifted upper lip, the quick twinkle in the grey eyes, which seemed to come irrepressibly, and half against the owner's will. When Betty scored a point—it really happened fairly often—it cheered her very much.

It was curious how much she liked Prudence Varley. She would have liked to see a great deal of her, not in the rarefied altitude of the studio, but in a more human and convivial atmosphere. She would very much have liked to ask her to tea (the Crevequers hated tea as a drink, but the function amused them, especially when they were the entertainers). She did suggest it one day, but Miss Varley, it seemed, had other engagements. Mrs. Venables came, with Miranda. Miranda was being educated; she was being introduced to the life of the people. The people did not interest her at all, but she liked the Crevequers, whose function was that of go-between. She would have liked to make a friend of Betty. She and Tommy were, of course, 'rotters'; they both talked much too much, and usually the most awful rubbish, and their absurd stammer made it sound sillier still, and you never knew when they meant a thing and when they didn't; and they neither knew nor cared anything about games or sport.

But, all this said, Miranda was left in an attitude of half-puzzled admiration, of which she could not have quite explained the reason. Her frequent 'I say, you are rotters, you two!' conveyed a little bewilderment, a touch of contempt, and an immense attraction. This attraction put Mrs. Venables into a position of rather annoying inconsistency. She was not strait-laced; she would have been beyond measure distressed had prudery, or any conventional limitations, been attributed to her—had she, in anyone's mind, been termed *bornée*.

Nevertheless, below her æsthetic self—the self which was struck, which designed Liberty dresses and wrote novels (those novels which the Crevequers had decided to put off reading till they were thirty-two and thirty-three)—there lurked a self more ordinary, to whom the artistic issues were obscured, who could become, on occasion, purely the disapproving, very reputable censor of conduct. It was the existence of this self, side by side with the other, which made Prudence Varley sit in judgment on her attitude towards the Crevequers and their kind; it was the existence of this self which made the position of Miranda something of a problem.

Theoretically, it was right and desirable that Miranda should see life as it was lived; practically, Mrs. Venables hesitated a little when confronted by the atmosphere so corrupt and so disreputable—she could not phrase it otherwise—in which Maddan Crevequer's children moved—an atmosphere that seemed to hang about them, jarring so incongruously, and at times (but not to Mrs. Venables) so laughably, with their great sad eyes and their flow of childlike nonsense.

So, half ashamed, Mrs. Venables held Miranda back from personal friendship, knowing herself false to her principles, and morbidly nervous of seeing the word *bornée* lurking behind her son's observing eyes. Seeing that it was expected of him, he occasionally made use of it; in protest against it she threw herself, and threw Miranda, with increased fervour, into the Intimate Contact with the People. In the Intimate Contact the Crevequers were links. To the club-room in the Vicolo de' Fiori (the steep alley next to that of the Crevequers) they induced their friends to come; on Tuesday evenings, from half-past six to half-past seven, girls and women (really a very creditable number) sat and made paper hats, and Mrs. Venables achieved intimacy with them. Then they danced; finally they paid a penny and had coffee and a bun, over which further intimacy was achieved. On Saturday nights men and boys came, and played bagatelle and spoof and quit, at Mrs. Venables' suggestion, and mora and *zecchinetto* on their own. The intimacy here was chiefly achieved by the Crevequers, who joined in the games. But every one was very agreeable to Mrs. Venables, though, as she said, difference of language (and of faith) made confidential relations a matter of slow growth. She envied the Crevequers their closer intimacy.

Miranda on these occasions usually sat in a chair by herself, looking about her with slightly aggrieved blue eyes. The faint disgust in the droop of her lips implied, 'Beastly place, I hate it.' She did not wish to achieve intimacy. She wished that Betty would come and talk to her, instead of playing with the People. Sometimes Mrs. Venables would command her to go and talk to someone; then she would rise reluctantly, feeling exceedingly conscious of her movements and quite over-large. The People, she thought, seemed mostly rather undersized.

'What's the good, Mother? You *know* I can't say a single thing.' Her voice dragged plaintively.

'It will be so good for you to try. Go to that nice-looking girl over there, making a petticoat. She is smiling at you.'

She certainly appeared to be doing so. The fact did not lessen Miranda's embarrassment. She waited till her mother turned away, then turned her back without ceremony on the nice-looking girl who smiled, and made for her retreat in the corner. There she sat, yawning dejectedly, till Betty Crevequer came to her. Betty stood in front of her, regarding her with a whimsical scrutiny, her head at an angle of contemplation, her lips twitching a little.

'Isn't it fun here?' she remarked. 'I knew you'd like it. Can you make paper hats?'

'Oh, I suppose so. Beastly things. I hate them.'

'Oh! I was afraid you might, perhaps. I was going to ask you to show some one how; but never mind. We're going to dance now. You wouldn't care to join, I expect?'

Miranda would not.

'I hate dancing. I say.'

'Yes?'

'Do you really like this? And how much more is there?'

'Of course; don't you? About a quarter of an hour more. Then there's coffee.' Beastly stuff. You'll hate it. I must go and dance.'

'There is certainly,' Mrs. Venables remarked, watching, 'something refreshingly picturesque in the movements of the Southern peoples. The lithe use of their limbs——'

She took in this impression with satisfaction.

'Don't think any of them can dance a bit, if you ask me,' Miranda pronounced.

The unwary remark drew her mother's attention upon her. Mrs. Venables' serious, fine eyes always seemed to weigh her daughter and to find her wanting.

'Dear Miranda, I wish you would try to take more interest in people. Miss Crevequer, now; she is entirely in their confidence, quite one of them, so to speak.' She turned to Betty. 'You must help this foolish child to a larger interest, and me to a deeper understanding. I have been having some most interesting conversations. I have been trying to glean from some of the girls their real attitude towards life in its deeper issues; but they are naturally reserved with foreigners—and, no doubt, with heretics. If one could convince them of one's very real sympathy——You are very close to them, one can see. You and I must have some long talks. And I suppose your brother has immense influence with the men and boys?'

'Well, they're just f-friends of ours,' Betty said, stammering a good deal, because she was tired.

There were times when the artist in Mrs. Venables sank a little in the helper; but here she ran up against a very blank inapprehensiveness. She had perforce to grasp that her uses in this capacity were purely financial. It is not easy to give to those who will not receive, who do not even apprehend their own need of gifts. This inapprehensiveness was as a blank wall; there was no surmounting it. They looked at each other from either side of a spiritual and social gulf; and the ignoring of its existence on the one side made any attempts at throwing, as it were, a rope across from the other impossible. The rope would have dangled—did dangle when experimentally thrown—ludicrously futile in mid-air. The thrower stepped back again to the artist's standpoint, and absorbed impressions.

To give financial help came to assume an aspect of immorality. Loans were gratefully taken, and no talk of repayment even remotely rose. It was, as Warren had put it, 'very obvious'—so obvious as to be tiresome. Illumination was shed on the aspect which the payment of debts presented to the Crevequers on the night when they came to dinner, in their redeemed dress-clothes, after winning on the lottery.

'And it all went,' Tommy concluded his narrative, stammering querulously, 'to a silly fool we owed money to. Wasn't it a shame, Mrs. Venables? We owed it him for months; he needn't have been in such a tearing hurry all of a sudden. Waste, wasn't it? All kinds of things, you know, we might have done with it. If we'd hired a motor-car, would you all have come to Pompei with us? Or would you rather have taken a boat to Capri? You could have had your choice, anyhow. And all that money wasted; we might just as well have dropped it into the sea, you know—

better; it would have been fun diving for it and bringing it up with our toes. Do you know how to do that, Venables? I did it once when a North German Lloyd was going out. You know how they swim round and dive for money and make such a horrid row? Well, I thought I'd do it, too, once, because it was such a nice warm day; and they threw me pennies, but another man always brought them up with his toes; I could never find them. Sell, wasn't it? but much funnier than paying all that money to Grollo. People are so grasping, aren't they.'

It was manifest that money lent to the Crevequers must be accounted a bad debt. Mrs. Venables lent no more; her moral sense rebelled against it.

But Warren proved himself admirably accommodating.

CHAPTER V
BAIÆ'S BAY

'I woke before the morning, I was happy all the day.'—R. L. Stevenson.

'Why should I care for the ages,
Because they are old and grey?
To me, like sudden laughter,
The stars are fresh and gay.
The world is a daring fancy,
And finished yesterday.'—G. K. Chesterton.

On a blue Sunday morning, not early enough to spoil their night—on principle they shunned always the dimmer hours of dawn—the Crevequers slipped the leash of the city and went to spend a happy day in the country. They often spent their Sundays thus; with their wonted inconsequent abruptness one would say to the other on Saturday evening, 'I'm tired of Naples. Let's go somewhere else by the next train,' and they would shovel a few things—usually those among their possessions which they were least likely to want—into a bag, and take tickets quite at random to any place, known or unknown, which occurred to them. Novelty was often a desirable qualification; but on this Sunday morning they went to Baja, because a strenuous week had blunted their imaginations; also, perhaps, a little because on the shores of Baja there lies much healing. Their affairs had not been going altogether smoothly of late, and the need rose in them, unworded, for stillness by blue water and the sun upon warm sand.

Having found these things, they entered into a contented peace, and built a sand castle. Then they lay on the sand ten yards from it, and took shots at it with bits of pumice-stone.

'Well,' Tommy observed at length, 'I've won that. And now it looks like a plum-pudding. Ducks and drakes? No; we'll go to sleep, because we got up too early for the time we went to bed. Pity; get up later next time. No, you can't talk yet, Betty, because I'm resting. You know, you don't need so much rest, because you're not a newspaper man. I'm sorry I'm a newspaper man; they're so untruthful, and when they try to be funny they're only rude. But I'm glad we're not a daily; if we were we should get into seven times as many rows as we do, shouldn't we. Our mortification might be greater than we could bear. Muzzi can bear a great deal, though; he's so brave. I'm not; I'm dreadfully sensitive. If I die a violent death at the hands of the Sindaco—I probably shall, you know, so will Muzzi—Mrs. Venables will have Masses said for me, because they're such an interesting medieval survival, obviously deeply rooted in human psychology. Why are heretics such goats? And why talk about heretics and newspapers on our happy Sunday in the country? Your turn, Betty; change the subject while I snatch a moment of sleep.'

Betty, her chin in her hands, was looking across the blue bay.

'I am thinking,' she said. 'No; I am absorbing impressions. They are illuminating and suggestive—quite striking. They really are, you know. Chiefly—Naples is there, and you and I are out here. To me at this moment that is very real and vivid—immensely significant. Perhaps I have expressed it badly, though.'

'Communicated myself inadequately,' Tommy lazily corrected.

Betty acknowledged his greater accuracy.

'But,' she added, after a moment, 'it was a real impression, all the same.'

She thought it over, looking across the bay towards Naples.

'Life in a populous city,' she murmured, after a moment, 'has its problems, its trials, its disappointments.... Mrs. Venables told me a story at tea the other day; I'll tell it to you if you like. There was a man once who had a lot of gold; at least, he supposed it was gold. It wasn't really; it was a base metal, most of it. Do you know what a base metal is? Well, anyhow, it's something that melts very easily when you put it into a fire. So he put it into the fire——'

'What an ass.'

'Yes; but don't interrupt. And he couldn't help putting it into the fire, because the fire is Life—it's an allegory, did I tell you?—and everything has to pass through it. Well, all his metal melted, and ran away, and he saw it had been nothing but a base metal after all. But one little bit he found which was pure gold; and that he kept, you see, always. But it was horribly disappointing for him that there wasn't more. When he was young he thought he had such a lot; that was where he was wrong. That's all that story. And Mrs. Venables says if we are lucky we may all end with a little piece of gold. Life, you see, is a smelting-furnace, a crucible for the testing of ultimate values.... Don't, Tommy, I can't bear it; I'll stop, really I will——'

She warded off with her arm an irritated shower of sand.

'That story didn't amuse me,' Tommy remarked resentfully. 'If that was the funniest thing Mrs. Venables said at tea yesterday, I'm sorry for you.'

'How shallow you are, Tommy. It wasn't meant to amuse you. And Mrs. Venables didn't make it up; she'd read it somewhere. Personally, I was wondering if there was anything in it. I told Mrs. Venables I thought it very striking. But you've got such a—such a *borné* mind. I've been trying not to be *bornée*; I don't believe you ever do. Never mind; now we'll go to sleep till it's time for Mass.'

It was very still on the beach and very warm, with the winter morning sunshine on the sand. Beneath the wide blue sky the pure blue sea stretched, with a little stir and glitter from the ruffling breeze that just rumpled the broad blue basin's edge, crisping and whitening it, making it tumble over with spurtling laughter, like a tiny child at play, and draw back lisping to comfort itself for its fall. Above the splashing and the little hushing draw, the church bells sounded from Baja, calling the bay to Mass. There was half an hour still for absorbing contentment on the warm sand.

To the right the castle blocked the blue sky, shutting the little bay. Across the wide waters to the east Pozzuoli loomed, transparent, jutting into the sea. Further, more transparent, delicately purple, Nisida seemed moored like a barge, with the point of Coroglio behind it. Coroglio shut the gulf, so that one could not see how behind it the bay swept down and ran to Naples. Naples was beyond the picture; the picture held only the blue January morning, with its glittering waters and brown sails and purple points and islands, and little waves that spurtled on warm sand, and behind the bells of Baja calling. There was also the salt smell of the sea, and the Crevequers, and their sand castle. These things, to Betty Crevequer, became suddenly, as Mrs. Venables would have said, very real, very vivid—in a manner all of life. She lay dreamily, her eyes narrowed to slits blue as the sea, absorbing the impression. Worded—but she did not word it now—it was, as she had put it, 'Naples is there, and you and I are out here.' Naples, set pink and white upon her shores, beyond the point, out of the picture, was life; and life, some one had said, was a smelting-furnace, a testing of ultimate values. Betty seemed to dream a dream—a dream of the testing of values by fire. She saw how it might be that metal ran away, melting in the flames ... how one might be cast up out of the fiery pit, taking with one the knowledge of pure gold, for what that wisdom might be worth. But perhaps also a little piece of it to keep—if one was fortunate.

And Betty shuddered at this vision of purging by fire, and at the 'mental standpoint' of the man who had conceived life so. One should be allowed to keep one's bright metal—gold or dross, it mattered little; one should be allowed to keep it to play with, not looking into its quality avariciously. There should be a ring set round it to guard it from the flames which might melt it away in one's hands. The melting of it would so horribly burn one's hands; and then there would be a blankness, and nothing left to play with any more.

It was at this moment that the 'impression' became of a great vividness. Life might be a furnace, but here were things untouched by its flame, cast up—so Betty saw them, with prospective eyes—out of the sea of fire on to the high shores. Here, by the edge of the sea, were she and Tommy and a sand-castle dotted with pumice-stone like a plum-pudding.... A swift moment of vivid intuition came to her, illuminating her vision of life, as she looked at Tommy, lying on his back, with his straw hat tilted over his eyes. She was lit by a flash of great certainty, of strange discernment.

The flash passed, and left her as one who wakes from a trance. She lay and looked at Tommy, and, looking, felt a desire for speech.

'I'm thinking, Tommy, that you're very lucky to have me to play with you, and that I'm rather lucky to have you to play with me.'

Tommy pushed his hat a little up from one eye, and turned a meditative and mildly surprised regard upon his sister. Her remark had had a flavour of unusualness. But he did not comment upon it; it was as if, in the momentary pause that followed his glance, something between them, very definite, very permanent in its existence, entirely unquestioned, because it had always been there, and hardly ever alluded to in words, because they were too close to each other and too unsentimental, took more definite and visible shape. Their friendship, their close comradeship, their affection, stood in that moment between them, recognized mutely of both. The kingdoms might fall, but that stood. Thus they did not word it to themselves; but, unformed, the knowledge illumined the consciousness of both.

But after that moment's pause Tommy returned to normalities.

'I grant you your luck; in fact, I might envy it you if I was less sweet-natured. Mine, of course, is less vividly striking, as Mrs. Venables would put it. But no matter; never be ungenerous on Sunday, and I'm glad you should have a happy life.'

Betty dragged him up forcibly by the hands, and they went up the beach to Mass in the little church. That illuminated moment of insight seemed to walk between them to the doors.

After Mass they went to the Albergo Vittoria, and had lunch on the terrace.

They talked then of the Venables. Betty said she had had her last sitting.

'I should like her to sit to me,' Tommy said; 'the way she stands, don't you know, with her head back'—the gesture of his own caught it not unsuccessfully—'and her eyes when she's going to smile. And the way her upper lip's so like her chin.'

Betty nodded. She, too, had gathered all that in the rarefied mountain air of the studio.

'I wish she'd come and see us, as the others do. Why doesn't she like us more?'

It was a simple question, thrown out casually and without much wondering; after all, every one cannot like everybody else.

But it was curious how Tommy grew abruptly red.

'How do you mean like us? I should think she does, doesn't she? Why — why shouldn't she?'

Betty's eyes consideringly took him in. He seemed, from his stammer grown aggressive, to feel an interest. Obviously he had been moved — moved a good deal—by 'the way she stands, don't you know, and her eyes when she's going to smile.'

'Well, you see,' Betty amended, 'she's too keen on her work, I expect, to want to see much of anyone. I dare say that's all.'

Tommy was a little appeased.

'She always talks a lot to me when I meet her.'

Betty's doubting eyebrows became a mark of interrogation. She demurred, not to the 'lot of talk,' but to the apportionment of it—the order, in fact, of the personal pronouns. Tommy frowned stubbornly, holding to it, and drank a glass of wine with a defiant regard over the brim. Betty, looking at him with puzzled eyes, at last shook a despairing head.

'No, Tommy, I can't; I can't imagine it. If you don't put it the other way round quickly, my brain will break with the effort.'

Tommy, between a frown and a reluctant laugh, lit a cigarette.

'Oh, don't rot.... And what's the odds, anyhow, as long as we're both interested?'

'I'm glad she's interested,' Betty said, reflectively striking a match. 'Then, they're all interested, which is nice. Mrs. Venables and Mr. Venables, and the baby Venables, (she loves us very much, did you know? Only she doesn't really think we're up to much, because we're rotters and we don't play hockey), and Miss Varley too. I'm glad we're so interesting, Tommy—aren't you? And now we've had lunch. We'll go in a boat next, I think. What a nice expensive lunch we've had! Let's pay for it.'

Then they took a fishing-boat with a large triangular sail, and turned and twisted about the bay, with erratic deviations of course and sudden heeling and recoveries. Then they landed, and lay again on the beach to dry in the afternoon sun, and played ducks and drakes, and composed limericks and wrote them on the sand with pieces of shell till it was time to go home.

But before this time Warren Venables had joined them. He had motored over from Naples to find them and bring them back with him.

'Of course we will,' Betty said; 'the road's much nicer, and it will take longer and save us our fares. We never get returns, in case anything should turn up, or we shouldn't be coming back or something. And we'll drive by turns; what fun!'

They stayed on the shore till the sky behind the castle glowed to a soft daffodil colour. Venables was a good companion; his limericks and his riddles and his anecdotes were nearly as silly, nearly as devoid of all point or relevance, as the Crevequers' own. He might have been capable, on occasion, of exercising a more grown-up and polished wit; but when he played with the Crevequers he admirably adapted himself to their young comprehension. He was a person of tact, when he chose to use it. He did not always choose. He had a habit—an insolent habit, his cousin called it—of wearing in his manner, plain to be read by the initiated, the shades of feeling which he merely did not think it worth while to hide better, because he relied, with careless, supercilious confidence, on the inapprehensiveness, the unreceptive blindness, of those with whom he came in contact. The world was, after all, in the main stupid; his own cleverness possibly sometimes overrated this stupidity; the swift enlightenment of a glance, the flash of some phrase, would occasionally rend his veil across and reveal him—even to the stupid—sitting, amused, contemptuous, discerning, behind his flimsy screen. This attitude, of lurking in careless concealment, his cousin characterized as insolent.

'One should try not to insult people's intelligence more than one can help, I suppose,' she would observe.

'Well, but when they haven't got any——Anyhow, we all do it; one's got to in polite life,' he would aver, defending himself.

'They've mostly got some; and if one's real self sits despising and criticizing, one's outer self has no business to be a decoy. Even if the real self keeps quite behind the screen, it's unfair; and if it keeps looking out, as yours does, it's insolent as well. You insult them by as good as saying, "It's not much of a screen, but it will do for you. If you do see behind it sometimes, it doesn't matter very much; and if the people looking on, who know me better, see behind all the time, it doesn't matter in the least." A screen, to be at all courteous, should be impenetrable both to the people concerned and to the lookers-on; and even then it's not honest—one should quite withdraw.'

'You know, if one quite withdrew from all the people one doesn't quite like, one's world would get very limited.'

'Well, yes'—she wrinkled her forehead in doubt—'only they should know the terms, that's all.'

It was probable that Miss Varley might have disapproved of the manner of the homeward journey in the motor, for the Crevequers, who were slightly inexperienced, drove, as they had suggested, by turns; and behind Venables' screen of serenity his real self undoubtedly watched anxiously, and occasionally looked out, betraying itself by the nervous tension of the hands waiting in readiness to seize the wheel; the screen was, indeed, rather insultingly flimsy. They ran along the white coast road, with the gold of the west behind them, and the pale blue winter sea beside them, and the bright city of many hues growing larger in front of them as they circled the bay. They went much too fast, and it was very amusing.

'You must show Baja to my mother sometime,' Venables said. 'She has only visited it with the native guides so far; and you will be able to tell her so much that's interesting and new—very new.'

Betty sighed after that renounced game.

'I'm afraid not, do you know.... Tommy, you awfully nearly slew that goat. And I'm sure it's my turn now.'

She had swerved from the subject with a laudable impulse of shame, her first in this matter. At the same time, she knew very well that Venables minded nothing; also, that if she had looked at him his amused eyes would have twinkled into hers. That she did not might have been taken to imply in her the rudiments of a growing conscience; or possibly of a feeling that, though she and Tommy might laugh at a person's mother, the person might well keep out of it. His not resenting it—but this she did not word to herself at all, for she would not for some time know it—showed that he accepted so much, easily and without surprise. Why resent that, of all things? it seemed to imply. It was, indeed, hardly worth a comment; it was so wholly in keeping; as he would have said, so obvious.

This easy, unsurprised acceptance of things as they were, in which Prudence Varley might have discovered insult, bore to the Crevequers no message, no implication. Their attitude towards such tolerance was the measure of their inapprehensiveness.

But, as Betty had had her moment of half-realization, so Tommy had his. Perhaps such moments came to the one whose turn to drive it was not, and who had therefore leisure to perceive. Tommy's moment came through *Marchese Peppino*. Betty observed, abstractedly, between fluctuating swerves and recoveries:

'Tommy's paper, you know ... has been getting into rows ... being sued for libel....'

Venables, his eyes on the road, his hand waiting in nervous readiness for emergency, said:

'Yes?... Mind that flock of goats.' It was, possibly, the distance of the flock of goats—quite two hundred yards—which partly gave Tommy his moment of enlightenment. Perhaps he had half known it before; anyhow, he took in freshly now that the large acceptance did not quite include *Marchese Peppino*. Even the tolerance of contempt has got, after all, to draw its line somewhere. Tommy almost took in, too, the slight lift of the brows, which might be taken to convey 'Does anyone really think it worth the sueing—that rag?' Venables himself had certainly the air of not thinking it, under any circumstances, in the least worth the sueing.

Tommy, his melancholy eyes on Venables' profile, faintly flushed.

CHAPTER VI
GRADONI

'Les clefs des portes sont perdues,
Il faut attendre, il faut attendre,
Les clefs sont tombées de la tour,
Il faut attendre, il faut attendre,
Il faut attendre d'autres jours....'—Maeterlinck.

There are steep streets called *gradoni*, which climb up from the old town below to the new town above; their slope is assisted by shallow steps at intervals. So shallow are the steps that you hardly notice each as you take it. Not until you arrive at the top and look down on the ascending way do you perceive how its climbing was assisted. Of like nature is the ascending alley of human penetration. At the top is the daylight; in the analogy, perceptiveness quite achieved.

In her ascending alley Betty should, by the end of February, have got far enough not to have taken Miranda Venables to lunch at the Trattoria Buonaventura with her friends Gina Lunelli and Morello, the painter. She met Miranda on Santa Lucia. Miranda remarked:

'I say, I'm jolly glad I've met you. I've lost Prudence. Mother sent me out with her to look at churches and things, because my ignorance is a disgrace, and Prudence stayed so long looking at some rotten mosaic things that I had to come out. Then we somehow missed each other, and I've been playing about alone. I say, I should think it would do if you showed me things, if I must see them. But there's nothing to see, is there? Nothing but the Aquarium, and I've seen that. Well, anyhow, I'll come round a bit with you, shall I, and then I can say I've seen something. Mother goes about with Murray; rotten book; I hate it. You haven't got it about you, have you?' she added suspiciously.

'No. You see, I'm a mine of information in myself. It is so nice to be well informed, isn't it?'

Miranda observed, between compliment and irony:

'You know an awful lot, I suppose.'

Betty nodded.

'One picks things up—one likes to learn. We might have a really instructive morning, only it's time for lunch. You'd better come and have lunch too. The Trattoria Buonaventura, in the Toledo—do you know it? No, probably not. I'm going to meet some friends there.'

'Well, I'll come. But it's only half-past twelve; it's a funny time for lunch.'

Betty supposed that it might seem so, remembering the breakfast at Parker's.

They went towards the Trattoria Buonaventura, and Betty pointed out objects cursorily, and, as a rule, with creditable veracity, by the way.

'The English church. Perhaps you know it, though? Is it nice inside?'

'No, it's not. But I don't like any churches; they're all stuffy. Mother keeps going to them, though she's an agnostic, you know. She hasn't got a religion—oh, I wasn't to say that; I mean she rejects dogmatic formulas—I think that's what she says. She won't let me reject them, because she says I'm not old enough to have thought it out yet.... What a funny place! Do you often come here? I love meals in restaurants, don't you?'

Miranda was introduced to Morello, the painter, whose ugly flexible face and expressive gestures set her wondering, and whose extraordinary skill at rapidly absorbing immense lengths of macaroni fascinated her. He talked with some vehemence, and did not seem to like to be interrupted. Betty, who never left anyone out, talked to Miranda, and acted as interpreter. The Signorina Lunelli ate and drank a great deal, and smiled with immense cheerfulness; Miranda admired her large beauty and fine physique very much. All three, she perceived, were great friends, not only with each other, but with nearly every one in the room. It was a very sociable and merry meal.

'You don't smoke, I think?' Betty said, as the coffee arrived.

'I don't mind trying,' Miranda replied. 'I was ill last time, but that was three years ago. I was a kid then; besides, it was a cigar of Warren's. Dare say I could manage a cigarette now.'

'Oh, I wouldn't,' Betty counselled.

After about a minute and a half, Miranda wholly agreed with her. Her feeling when she looked up and saw her brother at the door was sheer relief.

'I expect Warren's come for me,' she said, coughing out a cloud of smoke.

Warren had come for her. It seemed that Mrs. Venables was anxious.

'I knew this was your lunch-place,' he explained to Betty, 'and we guessed she might be with you. I'm sorry to interrupt—but you have finished, haven't you? My mother will be anxious, you see.'

Miranda rose rather shakily and said good-bye. She had quite decided not to take to smoking.

The aspect which the episode bore of the rescue of a truant child from corrupting company was not assisted, certainly, by look or speech. It was perhaps an aspect obvious enough to be left to itself, unaccentuated and unadorned. Rather, indeed, it required, for courtesy's sake, modification. Venables possibly intended to give it this. He had greeted Betty and Gina and Morello (he had met these two before) with pleasantness. He always was pleasant to the Crevequers' friends, though the screen was sometimes rather flimsy. He was not, it seemed, shocked or annoyed to find his young sister smoking in such a restaurant among such company—merely his mother was anxious. His face, as his eyes had passed from one to the other of his sister's companions, had been quite impassive. What gave to Betty such realization as she at the time got—it was not much—was mainly Mrs. Venables' anxiety, which must so hurriedly be appeased. Betty had not known Mrs. Venables for an anxious person; to be a fussing mother was to be *bornée*. But the suggestion was not aggressive. Partly the green tints of Miranda's round face served as a screen for the other elements in the situation. No one likes his sister to look sick in a restaurant.

So Venables informed Miranda as they drove to their hotel.

'It's not considered particularly good form, you know, to smoke in restaurants till you can do it fairly well. And, anyhow, that's not an especially elegant place to select for the purpose—or, for that matter, for any other purpose.'

'She always goes there,' Miranda returned limply.

Warren's eyebrows went up.

'Oh—she.... That's got nothing to do with you. Each lot of people's got its own resorts.'

'But, Warren, you like her, don't you?'

'Who is "her"? Miss Crevequer? What's that got to do with it? I only said she wasn't your sort. And if you want to know whether I like Signor Morello and Signorina Gina Lunelli, I can tell you I certainly don't. And your doing this sort of thing puts mother in a very awkward position; she won't know whether she can logically scold you or not. She sent you out to see things, didn't she? Well, you've seen them now, that's one thing—quite enough for one morning.'

Tommy, it seemed, had got his enjoyment out of the business. He had, he informed Betty, 'been helping Miss Varley to look for her cousin all over the place.' Miss Varley's version was, 'Mr. Crevequer came about with me; I don't know what use he thought he was, except to suggest quite impossible places, and to talk till I felt quite giddy with it. The way those absurd infants babble! And it's mostly such nonsense, when one listens to it; they always make me feel as if I was Alice and they were Tweedledum and Tweedledee; or perhaps the White Knight, because of the sort of gentle melancholy they've got. When they come to a meal it's exactly like the Mad Tea-Party. And it's so ridiculous the way, when one of them stops to stammer, the other finishes the remark, or goes on with it till the first one is ready again.'

Tommy's relations with Miss Varley had, during the past months, greatly interested him. As she so pleased him externally, it was natural that he should desire to make friends; and as this was an enterprise in which he was not used to fail, he embarked on it with some audacity. There was a certain detachment, lack of human interest, about Prudence Varley, as he saw her, which were to him merely walls to be knocked down. He set about razing them with cheerful serenity. It had certainly never occurred to him that, if he wished to make friends with anyone, he would have any difficulty in doing so. But the walls were rather solid, he found. Against the battering-rams of his light-hearted sociability and friendliness they seemed to stand firm; he was only occasionally cheered by 'her eyes when she's going to smile.'

He one evening came to dinner in a mood of reckless resolution; however uninterested, she should this one night be interested, more or less, in him; he would break through the guard somehow and 'achieve intimacy.' He skilfully arranged contiguity with her when they sat on the balcony after dinner and listened to the mandolins in the road below. To tune the scene to the note of seriousness he regarded as desirable—nonsense having failed—he was silent for an unusual minute, to let the night sink in: the broad stillness of the sea below the high road, with the moon cutting its silver lane across it; Naples curving round the water's edge, a great cluster of sparkling jewels; far off across the bay the red glowing column above Vesuvius, that flared and darkened and flared again. To the persistent tinkle of the mandolins below a tenor voice sang 'Addio, bella Napoli!'

Tommy, having given the impression its chance of absorption, inquired:

'Do you like it?'

She turned to him a little absently, and the glow across the water seemed to strike high-lights in her eyes.

'What?'

He swept his hand towards it.

'Naples—all that.'

'Yes.' She had a faculty of conveying all she meant by a simple affirmative or negative; it is, if one comes to think of it, a habit rather rare; most people supplement or qualify or explain. She added: 'The little of it I see. It's not much.'

Tommy enlarged; he would force personality into it.

'It's not my Naples. Mine is different.'

She assented, 'I know,' and he realized with triumph that she had accepted the personal element; she had hitherto always passed it blankly by.

'My Naples,' she said, 'isn't human; it's colour, and light and shadow, and the way the streets go—cut like deep gorges and climbing up—you know? I'm getting to know that a little. But that's Naples in one sense only—one meaning. The people who live in it I don't know.'

'You don't want to know them, do you?'

Having found the personal tack for once, Tommy adhered to it.

'Well— —'

Her considering silence seemed to discriminate delicately between the various types of 'the people who live in it.' It seemed that one might want to know some and not others.

'You don't care about knowing people, only things,' Tommy told her.

She accepted it in silence. Discrimination between 'people' would hardly, in the circumstances, have been courteous. Her next remark was a swerve, as usual, to 'things.'

'Oh, look there!... Some one told me it hadn't been so excited for years. I wonder if it means anything by it.'

Tommy left the achievement of further intimacy for another occasion. He meant to carry it through. That was a few days before he had 'helped her to look for her cousin all over the place.' During that search he had found her a little abstracted; she had not appeared to be listening to him much. Her habit of attending to him with a small portion of her mind only, if that, did not baulk him; it pricked him to renewed effort. The element of deliberateness in it passed, as so much passed, over his head.

But he partially caught it—he hardly could have missed it—on one occasion. That was on the first day of March. The steady strokes of the rain lashed the city, beginning with swift unexpectedness; the Crevequers, coming home from lunch, found Prudence Varley and Miranda at their door, delivering a note. They both looked very wet. The Crevequers, mournfully looking from under their large and disreputable umbrella—of all things they hated rain—felt an immense pity, a pity that would have seemed to Prudence disproportionate; she was used to present to the elements a tranquil inattention, and rather liked rain than not. Miranda, too, was of hard fibre; both, anyhow, were used to England. The Crevequers, from under the umbrella (they more than ever resembled Tweedledum and Tweedledee) said (in turns):

'Come up with us till it stops'—'You mustn't get any wetter just now'—'Or you'll be too wet'—'The only safe way is to get dry'—'In between'—'At the stove'—'We're so dull'—'We've no one to talk to; do come'—'Oh, but do'—'Well, anyhow, take the umbrella'—'We shan't want it; we never go out in the wet'—'We should hate to.'

The entirety of the failure of it all had pathos. Significance seemed to be suddenly brought by that failure into the fact that while three members of the Venables family had long been familiar with the room at the top of the pinkish house, the fourth had never set foot on the lowest of the stone stairs.

Tweedledum and Tweedledee went up to their room in silence.

It was then that the room seemed newly to become an impression to them; it was as if it had broken through barriers and suddenly pierced their senses. Their melancholy eyes took it in—a certain tawdriness it had, the litter of things incongruous: on the table a scattered pack of dingy cards; bottles and glasses, unwashed from last night, making red sticky circles on *Marchese Peppino*; everywhere was *Marchese Peppino*: one could not escape from it. From the half-painted, absurd ceiling to the stone floor stale air brooded, breathing of smoke and wine.

Betty thought suddenly of cold, rarefied air, with a faint smell of paint, and winter sunshine striking in through open windows.

Tommy said an odd thing, a thing it is possible he had never said before.

'W-what a beastly mess!'

Then he shoved a space for himself on the table, among glasses and papers, and began to make pictures for *Marchese Peppino*.

It was about this time, early in March, that the Crevequers took to quarrelling. It was a thing not usual with them, because they liked, of all things, a pleasant harmony. Rows, as they observed, made them feel ill. But at this time they developed a new touchiness; possibly Lent was partly accountable. Tommy wrangled with his editor, disputed truculently with the good-tempered Luli, assumed a mien of impertinent defiance towards his more urgent creditors, and snapped at Betty, who snapped back, and then they would stammer rude and unpleasant comments on each other for a minute or two—it took them longer to quarrel than it takes people who can fling their remarks unhaltingly straight from the lips—until one or other was ashamed and said:

'D-dry up.'

They quarrelled once about *Marchese Peppino*. Betty referred to it to Warren Venables, who, as usual, did not pursue the subject with enthusiasm. When Venables had left them, Tommy, sitting on the table with his hands in his pockets, looked down at his sister rather moodily.

'Wish you'd let my shop alone, Betty. Venables doesn't care a hang about it—can't you see?'

The surprise in Betty's melancholy eyes testified to the rarity of the ill-tempered tone; particularly it was rare from one of them to the other.

'Well—what does it matter, though?'

Tommy was frowning.

'It does. It bores him to hear about it. It doesn't amuse him; he doesn't think it's funny—and it's not particularly—and w-what's the good of making bores of ourselves?'

Betty regarded him thoughtfully.

'I don't think he's so easily bored as all that, you know.'

Tommy remained gloomy.

A curious element had come, just of late, into his relations with Venables—the element of embarrassment. How it began he could not have said, nor whence it sprang. It was unfortunate, as they saw so extremely much of Venables. More and more Tommy left him to Betty, refusing to make a third in their expeditions and amusements. Yet he liked Venables; he liked him as much as he had liked him at first, when the meeting face to face had carried him back curiously to the old days of school hero-worship. Now, for the last few weeks, he had become growingly silent in his presence; the difficulty of conversation made him rather angry; it was a difficulty he was unused to, and he could not account for it. It oppressed him, too, now, in Miss Varley's presence; the achievement of intimacy did not progress. Tommy supposed it might have something to do with Lent; Lent often affected one's spirits unfavourably. Life in general, in fact, was rather a bore. Tommy told Betty so.

'I'm tired of being overworked,' he remarked. 'I wish I wasn't a newspaper man. I wish I wrote novels, like Mrs. Venables. Let's write a novel, Betty. I wish I had a motor-car to play with, like Venables. I wish we were older, Betty—old enough to go home to Santa Caterina and live in peace on our hard-won earnings. Let's chuck it and go. We've got enough, if we leave our debts behind us, and eat like moderate Christians, and are out of reach of shops. What's the good of fooling here, and never having enough to live on, and—and——'

His stammer or his disgust choked the rest of his grievances from his lips.

Betty looked sympathetic.

'You'll feel better in the morning,' she said, 'if it's a fine day.'

She was standing by the open window, leaning out into the soft darkness. From the narrow steep alley below, and from the wide lit thoroughfare into which it ran, the cheerful revel of Naples at night hummed up.

'Let's come out,' said Betty, 'into the streets.'

And the two seekers after a quiet life strolled through the city together. They returned home a little after midnight, having made a very heroic and quite successful fight against care.

CHAPTER VII
RETROSPECT WITH THE SEARCH-LIGHT

'D'autres jours ouvriront les portes,
La forêt garde les verrous,
La forêt brûle autour de nous,
C'est la clarté des feuilles mortes,
Qui brûlent sur le seuil des portes....'—Maeterlinck.

At the end of the first week in March the Venables went to Sicily; they would stay there, probably, for the rest of the month.

'So for three weeks we shan't have a chance of eating too much at lunch,' Tommy remarked, on the evening after they had gone. 'Pity, isn't it? I loved those lunches.'

Betty nodded. She was feeling horribly flat. They both, that first evening, felt horribly flat. By the measure of their flatness they might have gauged the late immensity of their interest; there was revelation in it. To shake it off they went to their favourite gambling-place, and lost some money, and talked to some friends, and in general raised their spirits.

Something of this convivial nature they did every evening for a week. Then they stopped. Inexplicably, it was becoming boring. On the first night it had cheered them; on the second and third they had shut their eyes to the fact that they were bored; the other nights had been, growingly, of the nature of a fight against something—they could not have said what. It was something which seemed to grow, slowly, vaguely, yet with an irresistible sureness.

It is not during constant intercourse and association that influence gives birth to new comprehension. These fill the foreground; they loom too large in present interest to allow of a penetrating vision. The vision, the perception, the discernment, growing from vague abstractions to poignancy, come later, growing very slowly from seeds sown unnoticed. From the carelessly received seeds the plant pushes its gradual, painful way upwards, breaking the earth to make a place for itself, growing, perhaps, to be a tree, striking and spreading roots all through the upheaved soil.

So it began to be with the Crevequers. Absence and time began now their inevitable work. Atmosphere, doubtless at the time absorbed, but unconsciously, now sent its message from system to brain. Retrospect meant the slow beginnings of perception; therefore they fought against retrospect. What at the time had passed them serenely by, came back to memory in strange new lights. What at the time had been bewildering, put on, day by day, robes of increasingly translucent clearness. What at the time they had known, unheeding and uncaring, assumed a vividness quite new. With the accidentals of intercourse no longer overlaying, wrapping up and entangling the issues, these pushed a slow way out, and emerged at last, standing forth unconfused and unadorned, bald in their lucid simplicity.

Through the slow days and long nights retrospect gave birth thus to a glimmering perception; perception, its gropings not to be checked, to comprehension.

In the Crevequers' eyes the melancholy pondering grew more noticeable than before. Their brows sometimes drew together suddenly, as if, in the straying of their thoughts, they had lit upon something they did not like.

Of the Venables they spoke to each other less day by day. Each did not know how it fared with the other; each hardly knew how it fared with himself. It was well, perhaps, that during much of the day they had plenty to do. But there were the evenings. It was certainly a pity that they had begun to find convivial evenings so little amusing to them. Except when their friends came to see them they sat alone together. After a little while, when retrospect had taken them some way, they would often, by reading or talking, try to keep it at bay. But it was, at best, only a question of deferring; there remained always the nights. It was in the nights, of course, that retrospect most tyrannically had its way. The masterless nights are escaped steeds run loose for anybody's annexing. Retrospect annexed them, and rode them hard. In the nights, at all events, there is no confusing of issues, no foreground to obscure the vision.

It took a succession of nights and days for perception to reach full stature. Each, lying awake, or sitting together through the evenings while Tommy drew pictures for *Marchese Peppino*, caught new aspects of the things which moved in progression through their memory.

It seemed that each of the Venables family, marching through memory, flung at the Crevequers something which retrospect could turn into a ball for its game.

From Miranda Betty collected guileless remarks in inverted commas (some of the inverted commas Miranda had supplied, some Betty filled in now) as to 'different sorts of people,' and how each sort had its own conventions and its own resorts. Plaints, also, about liberty of association tampered with—Miranda was a veritable garden for such flowers. There was also that day at the Trattoria Buonaventura, with Warren Venables standing at the door, impassive, observing, unable to linger because his mother was anxious....

Then, in the procession, marched Mrs. Venables. Mrs. Venables had one day sloughed a self. She had not liked doing so; it was a self she valued; her most natural self, also—the æsthetic self, so easily and so deeply struck. From this self she had reluctantly emerged temporarily to stand forth a reputable, conventional Philistine—more, a maternal Philistine, of all creatures the most *bornée*. Driven by circumstances, she had talked to Betty Crevequer on the subject of friendship, its uses and abuses. A certain impersonal detachment she had used, choosing her words with careful discretion, to throw as much veil as might be over the maternal Philistinism. She had not wanted to hurt Betty, nor had she at all wanted that Betty should in her mind call her *bornée*. She might have been relieved to know that this was a word only in the Crevequers' vocabulary as culled second-hand from herself, and stored in the same carefully treasured category with 'standpoint' and 'forceful.' Not knowing this, she had really shown some self-sacrifice in taking her risks. To minimize them she had laid stress on the purely æsthetic protests that her taste made, leaving propriety aside. A certain refinement she herself exacted from those whom she selected for companionship—she began quite a long way off, in her anxiety for impersonal detachment; how should Betty have grasped it?—and she would have others exact it too. If youth is to lower the value of the precious jewel, its friendship, bringing it down to common—very common—earth, youth will inevitably be the poorer. There is, after all, something in the belief so widely current about touching pitch.... To lounge about the streets—to be exact, outside the doors of a theatre—at midnight, in company with people of the stamp of Betty's companions of last night— —

'Gina?' Betty had wondered. 'And Luli? But— —'

The mournful pondering of her eyes was rather inscrutable. It might possibly refer to the Achievement of Intimate Contact, which must Shun Nothing.

Mrs. Venables had suddenly at this point dropped the artist self to her feet, and risen out of it for a moment entirely, becoming purely the reputable, conventional, disapproving mother. She had said a most *borné* thing.

'It looked very strange last night. The Essingtons—the friends I was with—did not know what to think.'

The allusion, with that, had seemed to her to have attained enough personality to be safely left. The kernel of the matter, which, wrapped up delicately in æsthetic abstractions, was, 'My son must not do that sort of thing,' had been, in the speaker's eyes, almost too manifestly reached. Mrs. Venables had meandered away among the wrappings. It might have been necessary, but the consciousness of having said that anything 'looked very strange' had oppressed her. It had really been uncharacteristic. The phrase, of such an immeasurable depth of crudeness, must have been somewhere innate in her, passed down from a long line of reputable ancestors, and it had leaped out without her volition. She had endeavoured to retire from it, to wrap it up.

It was perhaps unfortunate for her that at the time she had quite succeeded. Or, rather, the kernel of the thing, so extremely plain to Mrs. Venables, had not been reached by Betty at all. She had been willing to admit that to lounge in the streets so late had, perhaps, looked strange. It was an admission very simple, and not at all galling. Against the use of the word 'pitch' to describe Gina Lunelli and Luli (she had quite missed any ambiguity there might be in its use, and had accepted, naturally, the assumption, put forward on the surface, that Tommy and she were the touchers, who might be defiled) she had protested:

'You see, we're all quite the same sort of people—Tommy and I and they. There's no difference. You can't—you can't separate us.'

Retrospect remarked that Mrs. Venables had not really, with any great determination, tried to do so.

Yet even then Betty's words had seemed to imply that she had begun, however vaguely, to discriminate between one 'sort of person' and another. Retrospect now completed that discrimination. Retrospect gave her, in plain language, the kernel, so carefully wrapped up, which Mrs. Venables had thought she could scarcely have missed. It was laid now in her hands for her to look at; she looked at it, missing nothing.

Retrospect pushed Mrs. Venables aside, having quite elucidated her, and showed in turn Warren. It painted him outside the theatre, in a difficult position—the Essingtons and his mother on one side of the picture, Gina and Luli and Betty Crevequer on the other. The picture was not without its instructiveness. In an awkward position Warren had relied, with the careless confidence his cousin termed insolent, on the obtuseness which saw nothing. His confidence was justified; the obtuseness had still seen nothing. He had not, probably, taken retrospect into account, or he might have adopted another course; he might either have turned his back on the Essingtons and his mother, or even—but this would hardly have been feasible—have introduced his companions into their company. In the course he did take, the Essingtons thought he showed good taste and a proper sense of the fitness of things.

Gina and Luli and Betty were no authorities on taste or the fitness of things.

Warren was everywhere; retrospect, exploiting him, never came to an end. It was strange, it was marvellous, how it was possible to miss things—things that so stared one in the face. Yet, how should one have known? There was no reason why one should know now; only the slow pervasion of atmosphere, that enabled one to look at things with such strangely new eyes, the eyes, doubtless, of others, with the added illumination of the subjective standpoint. This illumination shed its fiery light, growing from glimmer to flame through the masterless nights, upon the things Warren had said and done, the things they had done together, the things he would not have suggested, not contemplated even in thought, if he had regarded her as one of his own 'sort of people,' sharing his conventions. Who should blame him? He had been adequately justified; she had shown herself from the very outset—he had no doubt waited to be sure of it, so as not to risk insult—of a sort of people immeasurably different: so different that she had not even grasped the difference, had only not been surprised at hints of it because they had passed her so serenely by. They had passed clear over her head; dragged back through space by retrospect, they struck her full in the face.

She saw, in the blinding light of an illuminative moment, Warren's attitude towards a girl placed by him among his own 'sort of people'; she saw him brushing aside, lest they should touch and smirch her, the Ginas, the Morellos, the Lulis, who might have crossed her path; she saw his considerate respect, his equal comradeship.

She had given him no chance of respecting her, had he tried to do so. The things crowded back.... On the evening after the first lunch-party he had met her in the street alone at midnight. He had walked home with her; she read into his manner now a touch of the protective regard that she imagined in him towards his own sort. But it had been tinged with uncertainty; even then he had probably known her. Not to risk misjudging her, however, he had walked with her to her home, assuming, doubtfully, that she had lost her escort.

It had not taken many days to confirm the doubt, to obviate all necessity for such assumption.

And then—how they had played together! Each had been so contented with the other; they had had such fun. Retrospect with the search-light could not quite spoil that—not all of it. But it did its best; it dragged it through the mud till it was hidden, inches deep.

Prudence Varley would have seen a flimsy screen toppling over with a crash, revealing the lurker behind with his contemptuous smile. So Betty too very bitterly saw him: but she was aware also that the smile was not all contempt. Only the contempt, real or imagined, poisoned the rest.

The search-light flashed over the large, tolerant acceptance, so unsurprised, so unremonstrating, so uncriticizing, which had at the time missed its message. It did not miss now. She saw herself accepted, Tommy accepted, their friends accepted; all the things they did, their ways of life, taken easily, without surprise, with scorn lurking behind the screen. Their unpaid debts, and eluded duns; their disreputable haunts, their more disreputable friends, their street-loafing, their very dress.... Even at the outset Tommy had said: 'We don't dress well enough. I want a new hat; so do you.' So that obvious discrimination between 'sorts of people' their elementary perceptions had made at once; they had reached just up to that, and no higher.

The question of discrimination brought the quick question, What share of the gift had the Venables? For there were discriminations that might be made, between the things that the Crevequers had done, and other things that they had not done—things from which they had been kept, perhaps, less by any code, moral or conventional, than by the inherent force of inherited tendency, which, strike what new and individual roads we will, will not cease to follow us along them. The question of the discriminating powers of the Venables Betty left. She simply did not know.

All the time, while the search-light glared over the things that Warren had said and done, there remained, outlined lucidly against the background, the things that Prudence Varley had not said and not done. She, with her tacit omissions, was the influence almost preponderating. Her atmosphere was the most deeply absorbed—the rarefied atmosphere of the studio. Across the gulf of months Betty met the direct, far-seeing look, which took in all and gave out nothing. It had waited for its interpretation till now.

With the interpretation—which was that of things held back, reserved—Betty came to evolve a discrimination. The discrimination was between two attitudes. Both had held back something; neither had given unreservedly. One had held back all of friendship, offering nothing; the other had given friendship, withholding from it an element—the element of respect.

Retrospect made the most of both. It would have been hard to say which it found the more effectual weapon. There were moments when Betty could have caught at the sharp blade of one to escape the other, each was driven in alternately. Finally, in spite of all which she would have during these months foregone had she been taken at her word, in spite of all that retrospect with the search-light could not wholly spoil, she attained at times to endorsing the working principle of the entire withholder, as it had been once phrased by her—'One should quite withdraw.' Retrospect, on the whole, made it out a principle more honest, more kind.

Tommy, who was every day being shown a little more how Prudence Varley had from the beginning 'quite withdrawn,' concerned himself, not with the honesty or the kindness of the principle, but merely with its immediate basis.

So, coming to an understanding of its basis, he saw vividly his own hopelessly unachieved intimacy, his attempts so driven back upon themselves, yet gaily denying defeat, his battering at walls which had been built—not at all, as he had supposed, of abstraction, but of entire perception. He saw now more and more each day the impenetrability of those walls; retrospect illumined for him the unheeding detachment, the abrupt swerves from persons to things, so frequent because he had been so indomitable in his return to persons, perceiving them for gates in the impenetrable walls.

There had been times, there had been moments, when the gates had yielded a very little; one had, as it were, got sudden glimpses through. After all, the Crevequers had never failed, till now, to achieve any intimacy....

The half-conscious, vague knowledge of this made the shut gates the more significant; their barred faces were written over, large, with words. The Crevequers, having begun to learn to read, spelt them out.

Tommy's reading was perhaps attained to with greater slowness, greater difficulty—the fault of sex—than Betty's; but in the end the attainment was equally complete.

To Tommy one element in the business was all-important; before it the other elements shrivelled into nothing. But there were other elements which at times had their turn. There was the attitude of Venables, now realized as the basis of the embarrassment which had for some time been oddly, inexplicably, growing into their intercourse with each other. Wholly to absorb that attitude Tommy had to go back some years, to an old atmosphere—an atmosphere of discriminations between the things a man could do and the other things which he could not do. It is curious how environment can choke an atmosphere. This, of a certain social and moral decency, as evolved by youth in community, had been brought back to Tommy by Venables. Venables and the atmosphere reacted on each other; each explained the other. This was rather a question of the renewal of old things than of new acquirements. Four years—those four years—do not easily slip out of life. They had not slipped out of Tommy's; but it had needed Venables to make them stand and deliver their message. They delivered it, with whispers growing to clamour—a sordid recital of the things which a man cannot do. From the friendly inexpressiveness of Venables' eyes, Tommy gathered the classification 'just scum.' With a side glance at Betty's part in the business, he admitted that there were also, beyond doubt, the things which a girl cannot do—beyond doubt, too, Betty had done them; but here old atmosphere did not come to his help: his ignorance was as outer darkness. Those things were Betty's concern. He wondered a little what she made of them, if anything. He wondered a little also if he was angry with Venables; on the whole, it hardly seemed logical enough to be worth while. (Betty in this matter cut herself adrift from logic.)

Still nothing was said between them; still neither knew how it fared with the other. They, who shared all their thoughts, kept these thoughts locked from each other's sight.

Then, on the twenty-sixth of March, a letter was brought in to them as they sat over supper. They knew what it would say. The Venables had returned to Parker's—they would like to see the Crevequers at lunch the next day. Mrs. Venables was eager to resume the Intimate Contact with the People; she must have a talk with Betty about it.

Betty handed the note to Tommy, who was hunting in his pocket for matches to light his pipe. He glanced at it, then tore it neatly and with careful deliberation into strips, and folded them into lighters. Betty watched him; when he had done, he held one over the lamp and lit his pipe with it.

Having successfully carried out this operation, he turned to her.

'You didn't want it, did you?'

Betty shook her head. She had not wanted it at all.

Tommy got up and leaned out of the open window, his back to the room.

'I shall be busy to-morrow,' he remarked.

'So shall I,' Betty said slowly.

Tommy said presently:

'How much longer are they going to be in Naples?'

'Don't know,' said Betty, her chin in her hands. She was thinking it over.

Tommy said suddenly, 'Oh, confound!' and explained, after a moment, 'My pipe's gone out.'

They came thus to a perception of each other's position in the matter. By whatever steps this position had been attained, it stood clearly defined. Both were too busy to go to lunch at Parker's Hotel; that emerged saliently. With no words uttered on the subject, their points of view had marched together, side by side, immeasurable miles from the evening, three weeks ago, when one had said to the other, 'So for three weeks we shan't have a chance of eating too much at lunch. Pity, isn't it? I loved those lunches.'

The march of the other's point of view each accepted, silently, without surprise. The only matter for surprise would have been the march of one without the other. For, backwards or forwards, they had always moved side by side.

CHAPTER VIII
BROKEN BARRIERS

'The barriers break; life opens all about us;
The faces grown so long familiar are become as words,
Each one with infinite meanings, a new world.'—Henry Binns.

It was hard to deny Mrs. Venables entrance; her intimacy was so all-reaching. The Crevequers did not see how it was to be done. Betty almost reached the conclusion that it could not be done, and echoed Tommy's question, 'How much longer are they going to be in Naples?' In ignorance of the answer to that, the Crevequers built meanwhile their flimsy, pitiful wall, piling for bricks excuse upon excuse, lie upon lie.

Over the wall Mrs. Venables swept like a wave of the sea. She saw nothing; but, whatever she had seen, she would not have been deterred, but the more impelled. When she did see—if ever she saw—it would be an impression of the first order, most immensely striking.

What she at present saw was that the Crevequers had become unsociable; three weeks had been enough to throw them so entirely back upon their old friends and their old amusements that the new friends, with their atmosphere so widely different, had slid to a great distance, and were not welcomed.

'Atmosphere counts for a good deal. We have not, perhaps, made allowance enough for the strain—for it is a strain—of stepping out of one atmosphere into another. It takes time.'

Prudence Varley said:

'Only, when you don't step out at all, but carry your own atmosphere about with you, the strain is less. The Crevequers have always seemed, anyhow, to bear up under it.'

Since the Crevequers, finding the strain too great, refused to come to the atmosphere, the atmosphere came to them. It was carried by Mrs. Venables and Miranda; it spread itself over the sitting-room while Mrs. Venables talked. Mrs. Venables wanted another social evening in the Vicolo Fiori.

'Yes,' said Betty. 'I'll l-let people know.' (She was stammering horribly to-day.) 'But—but I'm afraid I shall be busy myself.'

Since the evening had not been specified, this was rather too manifestly a brick in the wall. Mrs. Venables pointed it out, with 'Every night, my dear?' and a lift of the brows.

Betty held to it.

'And—and every day as well. We're very busy just now, Tommy and I.'

They had become bored with the new atmosphere; they wanted to throw it wholly off, and be left in peace with their less reputable friends; this Mrs. Venables deduced, with displeasure now rising.

'I think,' she said, 'that it is to be regretted—very much to be regretted.'

Her tone dragged in to be regretted so very much more than the mere fact—the only one offered her—of the Crevequers' excess of occupation, that Betty's dark brows flickered nervously, resentfully, as if she feared something.

Miranda's round eyes beamed with sympathy. The desire to avoid another social evening with the very poor was wholly within the sphere of her comprehension.

'It's a rotten game; I hate it,' she observed.

Mrs. Venables spoke to her quite sharply for once on the subject of limitations of interest and ungracefulness of speech. Miranda, indeed, was a little in the way at the moment; she made intimate approach difficult.

Then Tommy came in, with Luli clinging to his arm. Both were so dishevelled, so flushed, so hilarious, that only one supposition was tenable. Mrs. Venables held it, and her eyes grew still more inclusive in their regret. She did not realize that it took really very little to excite the Crevequers and Luli.

Again Miranda was in the way. Betty realized it, looking, with the acquirements of her three weeks' retrospect in her pondering eyes, from one to another. It was not suitable that Miranda should be there. Betty, with the realization, achieved a fuller comprehension of the suitable than Mrs. Venables possessed; the thought amused her. Mrs. Venables caught the half-smile flickering to her eyes.

'The gulf of mirth,' she observed afterwards, 'is wider than the gulf of tears. One doubts if there is any bridge across it.'

The regret deepened in her eyes.

When Mrs. Venables had gone, and when Luli (much later) had gone also, Tommy said:

'What rot, Betty. What can we do to stop it?'

'Very little,' said Betty.

'It's such a bore,' Tommy explained. (They had not accepted the fact that their attitude towards the Venables could stand by itself, unexplained by one to the other. Unnecessarily, absurdly, each for the other's education piled bricks on the wall, with 'I'm busy,' or 'I'm bored.')

Tommy jingled the coins in his pockets, and whistled sombrely through his teeth.

'Venables been?' he said presently.

Betty's nod merely admitted the fact, without supplement or amplification. Nor did she state the exact number of times that Venables had 'been' during the past few days.

It seemed that they had now all been—all except Prudence Varley. The inadequacy of the wall was manifest; it kept out nothing.

Tommy, catching as he looked up a certain pinched look about Betty's lips, a strain of brows and forehead, a heaviness of lids, speculated again as to the extent of her realization of the things which a girl could not do; speculated also as to what, in the circumstances, would be one's attitude towards Warren Venables. He deduced resentment, and a desire for subsequent aloofness—a desire which might, perhaps, find itself at combat with other things.... Such a combat would hardly be pleasant; it would not conduce to restful nights. Betty did not look as if her nights were restful.

So much, in a moment snatched from egoism, the boy saw of the girl—saw uncertainly, with doubting divination, then returned upon himself, and, to flee from that, said:

'Come out. We'll get hold of somebody and come up to Vomero. I want a lark.'

The girl saw on the whole, perhaps, more of the boy. She saw, with tired compassion, a good deal of him. She saw how he shunned things (the facing of them had been forced on her, but not on him), yet how he too would probably face them eventually. When he had faced them, they would stand at the same point again; now she stood a little ahead. For she had faced things; there had been no shunning allowed to her. She faced them every day; she wondered in how many days she would be allowed to step on and turn her back upon them. If it was to be very many, what Mrs. Venables called the 'strain' might become rather oppressive.

As it happened, Tommy caught up Betty the next day, suddenly, and wholly unexpectedly to himself. He lunched with a friend on the Vomero; afterwards, being left by himself, he strolled through San Martino and came out on the belvedere. Prudence Varley was there, sketching. The leisureliness of her greeting seemed to take him for granted, to relegate him, almost, to part of the scenery. He speculated momentarily on the change in his own attitude towards this abstraction; how it had been to him once the absent remoteness of one interested mainly in things; how it was to him now the remoteness, not absent, but very deliberate, of one whose realization of and discrimination between 'sorts of people' was quite complete. It certainly might well have been clear to him from the first; there seemed no obscurity in it.

And here again they were together, looking over the spread of Naples. Before, he had swept his hand towards it and said, 'Do you like it?'

He had been pleased on that evening by what he had considered an advance, however slight, in the achievement of intimacy. He had flattered himself that she was slowly unbarring the gates. Once or twice, after that evening, he had, he had thought, induced the removal of a few more bars.

Now, standing outside the shut gates, having realized of what they were built, he flushed slowly to his forehead.

And then, even as he turned away, the old desire swept over him, ironically new in form. He would not batter at the gates again; that was done with. But he must, it was borne in upon him, show that he moved no more in the old mists of crass ignorance, show that he knew, even as she did, of the gates, their nature and their inexorability. That she should continue to think that he knew nothing was not to be borne.

So, turning, he checked himself, and stood still a little behind her, and looked down over the great tinted city circling the blue bay—her Naples, 'colour and light and shadow, and the way the streets go, cut like deep gorges, and climbing up.'

Looking over it, Tommy said, with surprising abruptness:

'You said once—or I said—that your Naples was different from mine.'

She glanced round at him for a moment, with her usual unadorned 'Yes.'

'And I didn't know then,' he went on, 'how much it was true. I think you perhaps knew I didn't know it. And now I should like you to know that I have learnt that much; that I'm not quite—not quite a b-blind ass. I know more or less how we stand—how we must always stand. That's all. I wanted you to know that I see them—all the things ... the things you've seen all along.... I wanted you to know.... Oh, there's nothing you can say....'

Thus the melancholy, stammering flow, till it, as usual, choked itself and died.

She heard it out in silence—as always. This silent hearing was the carrying out of what had from the first constituted their intercourse. For always he had talked and she had heard; Betty had once quite failed to accept Tommy's assertion that it was ever 'the other way round.' But the silence seemed now to hold a new element—the element of receptiveness. She listened wholly, swerving from nothing. It seemed that here was his triumph, long striven for; he had sounded the personal note and she had accepted it; in a manner, he had broken through the gates.

When the stammered flow broke, she continued the silence for a little. Then she assented to his last phrase, saying, very gently:

'No—I can't say anything. There is nothing to say.'

The sad, judicial candour of it set the seal on the position. If he had still wildly, faintly hoped that she had not, perhaps, seen so utterly 'how they stood, how they must always stand,' that hope died then. He had divined so much correctly; there might even, perhaps, be more of it, that it would take some years yet to divine.

The glow of the coloured city made his eyes ache as he looked.

He said again, what seemed to be the final expression of the situation between them, this time altering the pronoun:

'There is nothing I can say.'

All he might have said, all he now knew that he would have said, had they stood differently in each other's eyes, all that it would have been, as they did stand, an insolence to say, seemed to lie in the silence between them. Since she was (now) so receptive, she possibly took it in, or a little of it. But 'there is nothing to say' finally summed the situation.

Tommy stammered 'Good-bye,' and went.

The Crevequers had supper at home and alone together that evening. Over it Tommy said nothing at all, and Betty talked without a break for the edification of the two of them. After supper Tommy lit a pipe and began to work at some sketches. Betty, in the other arm-chair, counted pence in a money-box for the week's rent.

'It would be too much to expect that it should be right, of course,' she murmured, 'But w-why it should be eighty centesimi out, I can't understand.'

Then she looked up and met Tommy's eyes. All his sharp hurt was in them; they were heavy with a bitter, dumb hopelessness. If she had known it, her own eyes looked with the same heaviness, the same sharp hurt. The Crevequers were absurdly like each other just now.

'Eighty out,' Betty repeated, looking away from that other hurt. 'I can't—I can't understand——'

Unexpectedly, her voice broke on the words. Tears took her; she leaned her forehead on her hand. She was horribly tired of talking; she had talked all day—talked nonsense, stammering over it. She could not talk any more; the end of a tether often comes quite suddenly so.

Tommy looked at her gloomily, under his brows. Betty never cried; tears no more belonged to her than to him. When they had been children, one had hardly ever cried without the other. Tommy looked at Betty's tears now, speculating on her 'mental standpoint,' and on how far she divined his.

'What's wrong?' he asked. 'Anything ... I can do...?'

If it was merely the mental standpoint, he knew that she would not word it; so he exposed himself to her answer, unafraid. They had never failed each other by betraying such trust. The completeness of his trust enabled one to watch the other's tears without wincing.

'N-nothing,' said Betty, and her voice, in its weariness, caught upon a laugh, while her eyes were still wet. 'Only—only I think I've been talking too much to-day—and that's so tiring.' (It would seem that the Crevequers must lead an exhausting life.) 'And I met the baby Venables sitting outside a church, and it talked about beagling; you run after a hare till you catch it—did you know? It's so jolly. Thinking of that made me feel tired, I expect. And have you been stealing eighty out of the rent? Because I haven't.'

She was counting the pence again, laying them in precarious piles on the arm of her chair.

Tommy had gone to the window, and stood looking out into the soft darkness and the noisy street below, his hands in his pockets.

Those tears had somehow a little loosed his speech.

'The beastly thing,' he said drearily, 'is how everything is such a bore, and how it will go on always, just like this.'

Betty did not need him to tell her that that was a bad thing—one of them, but not the chief. She said:

'I know.'

'No; but you can't quite know,' Tommy told her, 'because—because for you it's rather different.'

The quick movement of Betty's hand sent the pence scattering on to the floor, ringing on the bare stone.

'There'll be more than eighty out now,' she said. 'And it's not different; it's quite the same.'

Tommy turned and faced her, pondering, looking at her from under gloomy brows, seeing how she had sunk her chin on to one clenched hand, and was looking down at the pennies on the floor sombrely. He was speculating on her position, how it could be quite the same. She elucidated it a little with, 'It's what one can take that counts ... nothing else.... So it's quite the same.'

Tommy thought it over, and said, 'I see.'

Yet it seemed to him that what one had been offered might also, in the long run, count a little—anyhow, in the retrospect.

Such an amount seemed to have been now admitted between them that Betty could say, 'We're down on our luck, you and I.... Tommy, I'm horribly sorry.'

The last was pity, and he took it from her now without wincing; that it was 'quite the same' for both of them made it a simple thing to give and take. He gave his in return, gently, now that her position had thus emerged to him.

'I'm sorry, too,' he said.

So their affection for each other put out reaching, groping fingers through the glooming mists of pain that blinded each. As yet that touch could not heal: but it seemed to wait its hour.

Tommy returned to his drawing. Betty sought for and gathered up the coins from the stone floor. Their copper jingling seemed to ring in her soul dully. The beastly thing—to use Tommy's phrase—was that one must oneself throw one's bright metal away. Though it might burn to the touch, the flinging of it away was a wrenching that hurt more. Betty envied Tommy, with the bitterness of his down-bent face before her; her bitterness must of necessity be the deeper, because her bright metal had been laid in her hands, to keep if she would. Also, to throw it away had bruised and hurt not her alone....

Betty's thin, scarred hand covered her lips, steadying them.

'We shall be better soon,' she said to herself. 'We'll play in the streets and smell the sea ... and summer's coming.... We shall be better soon.'

Then she sought a narcotic in literature, and got from the shelf a book of poetry and began to read:

'When you are out alone I hope
You will not meet the antelope....'

The Crevequers used often to cheer themselves with that book when they were in low spirits. But to-night it did not seem efficacious. Betty supposed she knew it too well; she could think as she read, which was not desirable. So she turned to fiction, and read 'Sea Urchins.'

The church clocks struck ten. Tommy, holding his sketch from him, said, 'How damned bad!' and tore it abruptly in two, muttering, 'Muzzi would if I didn't.' Then he got up and said, 'It's stifling in here. I shall go out.'

He went out.

Betty, her hand over her shaking lips, muttered, 'Poor Tommy—oh, poor Tommy! We've no luck at all, he and I.'

She was aware how he must have faced things, and how once more they stood at the same point.

CHAPTER IX
FURNACE FLAMES

'Ahi quanto a dir qual era è cosa dura
Questa selva selvaggia ed aspra è forte,
Che nel pensier rinnova la paura!
Tanto è amara, che poco è più morte:
Ma per trattar del ben ch' ivi trovai,
Dirò dell' altre cose, ch' io v' ho scorte.'—Dante.

Beneath the hail of black dust and fiery ashes that blew in gusts from Vesuvius across the bay, Tommy Crevequer screwed his eyes and tilted his straw hat forwards and drew, getting an excellent view, if not of Vesuvius, which was blotted in brown mist, at any rate of the population who thronged the harbour, and of the way in which they received their impressions. Foreigners—never-failing game—were much in evidence, a North German Lloyd having recently arrived; there were also the Sindaco, and various other celebrities. The artist of *Marchese Peppino* made them seem rather funny. It was the first morning after the breaking out of the eruption, and interest everywhere was vivid. Journalists recorded their impressions with smarting eyes.

A little way from Tommy, Warren Venables stood, a leaf torn from a sketch-book thrust beneath his hat to guard forehead and eyes. Tommy had seen him some time ago; he was rather bored when Venables looked round and saw him, and strolled towards him.

'Interesting,' said Venables concisely; and Tommy nodded.

Venables half looked over the artist's shoulder, with a careless 'May I see?'

Tommy shut his notebook with deliberation, and put his pencil into his pocket. Then, after a moment's interval, he flushed, slowly and with great completeness.

'You know it's a rotten rag,' he said, hurling down the other's screen with an angry blow that sent it crashing in pieces.

Venables, looking at his resentment for a moment in silence, said simply:

'I beg your pardon, Crevequer.'

He, too, had flushed. He was learning, it seemed, the 'insolent flimsiness' (as Prudence had it) of all his screens, this among the rest. He wondered for how long Crevequer had known that he 'knew it was a rotten rag'—or, rather, for how long he had cared.

The red, fine ash drifted before a push of wind into Tommy's eyes and mouth; his sullen anger surged in him, and broke stammeringly out. Inconsequently, he was glad to see how the soft, drifting dust lay on Venables' coat and very clean collar.

'You thought—you thought I—we—didn't know a thing about it, or about anything else, all this time. Well, w-what business was it of yours? and—and why couldn't you have let us alone?' Querulously he stuttered it out, and coughed out the dust as he ended.

Venables said again, 'I beg your pardon.'

Tommy glowered at him resentfully.

'That's no good. You—you had no business....'

His own outbreak had taken him by surprise. He was seeing the pinched look round Betty's lips, the strained heaviness of her eyes.

Venables, his quiet face very inexpressive beneath the paper guard, said, 'No, possibly not;' and that again took Tommy by surprise.

His flare of anger flickered down to a sullen smoulder; it seemed to lack fuel. Venables' silence, as they stood together, seemed to put him, as usual, in the right. After all, though 'what one can take' may be the only thing that counts on one side, what has been offered can hardly be left out of a sane vision of the other. Tommy, resentfully aware of this, was stirred to surprise, not for the first time, at the part latterly played by Venables in this matter. It seemed hardly characteristic; a certain reckless unwisdom it had, which was incongruous. Tommy wondered whether it was that play had at last grown suddenly to earnest, an irresistible tide swamping judgment, or whether this late development might perhaps be sheer amends.

Anyhow, now, since Venables, from whatever motive, had thus done the decent thing, they were again seas apart. Venables had, in a manner, by doing the things which retrospect had exhibited to the Crevequers as not quite decent, come down for a little to their level. It had only been for a little; he had now regained his own. His apology for his descent set him there with more entire security than before.

Tommy, as they stood together, wished—he had of late wished it a good deal—that he liked Venables less. It was that element in any relationship that made the difference of plane oppressive.

Venables, who had been standing in considering silence, seemed to remember that there was very little left to say between them. He nodded good-bye, and turned away.

Tommy slowly opened his notebook, and stared at his half-completed sketch beneath drawn-down brows.

'What rot; what sickening rot,' he murmured, and finished the drawing with quick, skilful strokes.

This was a great time for newspaper men. Leaving the harbour, Tommy strolled into the town, to seek impressions. The most vivid, coming to him unsought, was one of cinders and black dust falling like intermittent rain into his eyes. To protect them he followed Venables' example, and thrust a page from his sketch-book under his hat. In the street outside Santa Chiara he encountered Mrs. Venables and Miranda; they were coming out of the church. Beneath her swathing motor veil, Mrs. Venables' face was alight with exaltation. She also, manifestly, was seeking—and finding—impressions. She accosted Tommy.

'Immensely striking.... But too pitiful'—she indicated the church—'the prayers, the unreasoning, childlike terror. In the streets, too, the poor terrified refugees, clasping their household gods and lighting candles to the saints as they walk ... infinitely pathetic ... if one could tell them how futile!'

She paused, remembering, perhaps, that Tommy, as belonging to the same childlike faith, might also, on occasion, light a candle to the saints.

'It seems a natural thing to try, under the circumstances,' he remarked, confirming her suspicion.

'Poor souls,' she murmured. 'I must get over to Bosco Trecase to-morrow.... Human nature in the raw ... deeply impressive. One's heart bleeds for all the broken-up homes. And the way they take it—children hurt without knowing why. That seems to me to be infinitely pathetic; don't you think so, Mr. Crevequer?'

Mr. Crevequer tapped his sketch-book with his pencil. The difference of plane did not oppress him particularly in Mrs. Venables' presence; he still almost enjoyed it.

'It's got, you know, to seem f-funny to me,' he explained. 'But I admit it's a little forced, some of the humour.'

'Oh yes—your paper.'

Mrs. Venables became vague; her eyes greedily took in impressions from the passers-by.

Miranda said, 'Oh, I say, do let's see!'

Tommy did not open his book. He changed the subject.

'Rather pretty, the way the cinders fall, don't you think?'

Miranda said that the atmosphere was beastly, and that she hated it.

'It gets right inside my clothes—all gritty.' She wriggled distressfully. 'And my shoes are quite full of it. I want to go home to lunch, but mother won't. Mother likes it, I believe.'

'The worst, I am afraid, may be still to come,' Mrs. Venables murmured. 'They say we may expect a terrible night. There are sinister omens....'

'Oh, it is a rotten place,' said Miranda, disgusted.

It grew to be so, more and more, through the day. Tommy met Betty for lunch, then continued his impression-seeking, coated from head to foot in black dust. They arranged to be in for supper at eight. Betty was not surprised when Tommy failed to appear; there was so much of increasing interest going on. Instead, Gina Lunelli came in, seeking cheerful society because she was horribly afraid, with the abandoned physical terror of large, full-blooded people. The Crevequers always cheered one, made one laugh; she sought them, therefore, and found Betty alone, waiting for supper.

Supper restored Gina a little; she became more cheerful, though still observing that there seemed every probability of the world coming to an end in the course of the night.

'The way it blazes—Madre Dio! And the ashes that choke one! And this horrible storm! And Tommy—he's out in it!'

'Oh, Tommy's all right.'

Gina shrugged her broad shoulders.

'What with the storm, and the ashes they're shovelling in great heaps off the roofs, and the wild people there are about, and no one to keep order, and the convulsion of the earth.... But who knows? We must hope for the best, and the saints are good.'

Later on in the evening there actually was a slight convulsion of the earth. It shook the furniture and made a rattling, and caused Gina to have a fit of hysteria, and sent her running out into the street, notwithstanding the storm, averring that she would on the whole prefer to be slain by lightning than by a collapsing roof.

Betty curled herself up in her chair and listened to the voices of the night. It was about eleven o'clock then—a black, wild night, full of the storm. The earth growled back strange mutterings in answer to the rumblings of the sky. It was as if all hell was loose, and playing about Naples that night. The thunder-peals and the answering earth-growls grew in reverberance, in sullen rage.

Betty wanted Tommy.

There might be many reasons, but there seemed on the face of it to be no reason, why he should not have come in. He had probably been asked to supper by some one. But he had said, for certain, that he would come home.... Betty did not think that Tommy had lately been in a mood to seek sociable evenings with friends.

Gina's terror, the wild night, the storm in the air, caught hold of Betty with an insistent grip. The voice of the travailing earth played on her strung nerves as if they had been banjo-strings. She smoked cigarettes to still them; she tried to read, to ignore them.

A little after midnight the city shook with great definiteness. The room quivered and rattled from floor to ceiling. Betty, after that, went out into the streets, to see how things were, to meet other people, to find Tommy, to escape her own society. The Crevequers were gregarious; they on all occasions sought other people's society in preference to their own.

Betty was in the fashion; every one seemed, upon that upheaval, to have sought the open, more or less regardless of whether or not they were clad suitably to face it. Some of them were not at all clad suitably; they gave an impression of extreme haste. Close to Betty a stout lady in a nightdress shivered, and clasped a whimpering pug in her arms.

There was an influx into the churches; there was crying and moaning and telling of beads. An impromptu procession passed, bearing lighted candles, and a wax San Gennaro lent from his altar by his *parocco*.

Meanwhile the mountain across the bay flung into the black night its glowing masses. Above it hung an immense fiery pillar, blazing across the dark, restless sea.

Vesuvius had not done yet.

Betty looked for Tommy.

She did not find him; she found instead Mrs. Venables, and thought, with a vague, detached part of her mind, what an orgie this must be.

Mrs. Venables was not pleased with Betty, but the strikingness of the present occasion seemed to unite them.

'Deeply impressive.... I suppose few of us have ever experienced such a night.... I am going into the church.'

'I'm l-looking for Tommy,' Betty said mechanically, staring down the street.

Mrs. Venables did not hear; she was borne away by the crowd, murmuring, 'The city of dreadful night,' the light of exaltation kindling her fine plain face.

'But probably he's home by now,' Betty suddenly thought, and pressed a way through the people to her own street, and climbed the black stairs to the small room, where the lamp flickered dimly and nothing else moved.

Betty huddled again into her own arm-chair, and rested her chin on her drawn-up knees, and stared across at the empty chair opposite her. She wanted Tommy; Tommy who would so have talked if he had been there— the last more silent weeks had slipped from memory; Tommy, who was so often late in returning, who might be occupied in so many ways during this strange night, yet whose absence, nevertheless, grew with the hours to have a sinister meaning, as well as an infinite solitary sadness.

The storm rolled over Naples.

CHAPTER X
BETTY AND TOMMY

'So flesh
Conjures tempest-flails to thresh
Good from worthless. Some clear lamps
Light it; more of dead marsh-damps.'—George Meredith.

Through the black, slow hours Betty stared with wide unswerving eyes at the other arm-chair. On one of its arms lay a pipe, on the other a half-finished drawing. Between them, it was strange how Tommy sat, drawing, with face bent down, saying nothing. His presence grew, till the loneliness of the room was conquered. How should it be lonely? It held, as always, a companionship of two. As always, one had only to look up to see the other. So had all the past been; so would all the future be. No other state was within the bounds of imagination. As Betty once, at Baja by the sea, had looked up swiftly and seen, for life and all it meant, all it contained, herself and Tommy on warm sand, and a sand-castle dotted with pumice-stone like a plum-pudding, and had then been lit by a flash of vivid insight, of great certainty; so now she came, by slower steps, through the black night to the same realization. For it was after all a thing always known, if unexpressed, this companionship of two which should endure, stronger than death, surer than the thing called love, failing nowhere. It had been from the dawn of the days.

To the further north there lay, in sunshine, a little warm bay of blue sea, and a Ligurian fishing-city, pink and yellow and white and green, was set curving round it—Santa Caterina, of deep stone-paved streets, where odours dwelt of roasting coffee, and drying fish, and cheese, and drains, and tar, and the breath of the brown seaweed, and of the nets that had drawn in shoals of *bianchetti* at daybreak, and lay through the day drying on the hot sands.

A town of people most companionable, who played a kind of croquet (it is more amusing than ordinary croquet; you kneel in the road, and use boards for mallets) in the piazzas, and along the dusty roads where the white walls shaded them; who sat and talked outside the church on Sunday mornings, while their women tied their handkerchiefs over their heads and went in to Mass. During Mass the sweetness of the church smothered the saltness of the sea, but when the church-goers came out again into the hot piazza the sea's breath caught theirs, stealing up to meet them, calling most insistently, through deep little arches, that framed blue glimpses like pictures in a row. Going down on to the shore—it lay just outside the stone streets—one saw how, from the point of Savona in the west, across to the white gleaming of Genoa, the city of ships, all the blue bay stretched. Down by the tideless still edge of it a white canoe with a red stripe waited—a canoe for two (but it held five quite nicely, if some one sat astride on each end, so that its owners, being sociably inclined, sometimes took parties of friends).

In the canoe the owners came to Mass, from their house at the very end of the long town, well outside the stone streets, with a stretch of white dusty road to be traversed, unless they took the sea-way. Paddling back across the bay, the canoe landed beneath a little square, dark red house, with green shutters and a wide veranda and a small sweet-smelling garden of close-crowded flowers—roses and tall lilies and evening primroses; and for the trees, oranges and lemons, pomegranates, and fragrant eucalyptus, and fluttering bamboos, with vine trellises overhead. The house stood literally on the seashore, so that when the waves were high they came in through the green iron bars of the gate and washed the growing things with brine. On one memorable occasion they flowed in through the basement windows; the exultant household then went downstairs and floated about on tubs.

Inside, the house was artistic, in an unconventional way of its own; its owner had been called an eccentric of genius. He had been a lovable person, wrapped in his own thoughts and his own work, giving his children most of the things it occurred to them to demand, spoiling them entirely, and leaving them for the rest to shift for themselves, which they did, with infinite enjoyment, on the sea and on the hills, and chiefly in the companionable streets of the town, where they played in the piazza and talked in the *farmacia*, and loved many friends, and learnt the art of how to be happy though doing nothing.

No one inquired after their movements, except on occasional mornings when it occurred to the master of the house that he would teach them something. Even then they had all the hot afternoons and long, still evenings for their own, with a warm, happy, gay world to play in, with rocks half a mile up the shore, where the white canoe paddled about and turned over suddenly in the warm water (one then navigated it upside down, which was quite as agreeable), with the cheerful town waiting always; and just behind the house steep hills of silver olive-gardens, walling the bay from the trans-Apennine winds.

Climbing the stony paths that led straight up from the stone streets of the town, one passed through gardens of oranges and sweet-smelling lemons and long vineyards, and above the grey olive terraces and chestnut woods, to the place of rocks and dark cypresses and green stone-pines. Up there was a little lake of deep green water, with red pine-bark lying in heaps by the edge, so that one made boats and raced them across.

Thus, however much the Crevequers enjoyed the kind, gay and amusing world—and they enjoyed it, as a rule, tremendously—they were always aware that there was a better place waiting for them. Some day they meant to go back there for good, in the days of repose that age should bring them, and live together in the house beyond the long town (it belonged to them; they had little other heritage), and cross the bay in the canoe with the red stripe, that lay in the basement now and horribly needed caulking, and land on the beach below the little city, and go up to Mass in Sant' Ambrogio, and afterwards play games in the piazza and sit outside the *parrucchiere's* in the sun.

They had left Santa Caterina ten years ago; a sudden pricking of duty had come to the hermit of the red house; his obedience to it had, as Mrs. Venables said, cost him his life shortly afterwards.

Three most forlorn things Betty had in her memory, following on each other: the leaving of Santa Caterina, Tommy's going away to school, and the death, a year later, of the careless, indulgent eccentric. At the first and last she and Tommy had wept together pitifully; at the middle tragedy of the three the iron had entered into her soul, too deep for tears. It had mattered infinitely most.

But there had been, through those four years, the holidays—holidays mostly spent in an untrammelled and lawless liberty in London, with a light-hearted and irresponsible old Irish gentleman, their grandfather. It was in those days that they learnt to love the glamour of a great city. London they had known, as they now knew Naples, with a vagabond intimacy for the most part denied to the children of their class. The gamin strain that seemed innate in their blood was developed and strengthened thus.

Part of these years had been spent with a family of cousins in a country vicarage. The memory of this portion of their career still lay like a heavy load on the Crevequers' consciousness. The atmosphere—an atmosphere, one would think, of fairly ordinary respectability—had not till then come their way. They stifled under it. No one in the household but themselves was in the least degree foolish, and they, being frankly babyish, and quite disreputable in their tastes, were more than ever driven to one another, facing the rest of the world hand-in-hand, hopelessly recognizing the impossibility of explanations, hopelessly failing to arrive at any perception of the civilized and usual code. It was to them merely an oppression, but from the oppression each had the other to fall back upon, and they were content. But, notwithstanding the smothering weight of civilization, they had always, even in those days, got on extremely amicably with the world in general. The failure to achieve friendship had not entered into their view of life as it was lived by them. That was a thing they had had to learn later, and at first with blank non-comprehension.

The little of decency that had in these days penetrated into them—no one can quite escape the impress of the educative years—had during their life in Naples slipped quite out of sight. In Naples they had entered into a feckless, laughing world, where they had lived from hand to mouth, and made friends in every street, and 'drifted about the bottom.' So drifting, they had been still together. For that reason everything had so greatly amused them; jests coming their way had, in passing from the eyes of one to the eyes of the other, acquired an overpowering humour; the world had been a merry playroom for two. Any friend made by one of them had been introduced, as a matter of course, into a three-cornered party; no other way could ever have occurred to either.

And now, out of life the crucible, immutable values seemed to evolve themselves. That story which Tommy had found so tedious on the beach at Baja had been fulfilling itself of late. Life had truly proved a furnace, whose pitiless flames melted one's bright metal and horribly burnt one's hands.

Those who in the end emerged from that furnace would certainly know their metal for what it was. Betty, still in the flames, could look ahead: she saw with increasing clearness the result of that testing and the gold that would remain—gold that could not, by any alchemy of newly acquired knowledge, be proved base.

But if one lost that gold, then life—the essential interpretation of it— would end there. It were better that the name of it—the poor kernelless shell—should be swiftly crushed too. It would, no doubt, find itself crushed somehow before long, because no continuance of it was in the least degree imaginable. One cannot separate two lives so tied together.

So, through the slow hours, life resolved itself into certainties, that rose like sharp rocks out of the mists of doubt. With their increasing clearness of outline, the emptiness of the other arm-chair became a jarring outrage; it was as if, to one who has learnt to say, 'This one thing matters, this one thing I must have,' the curt reply is flung, 'This one thing for the present you must go lacking.' The solitude became an offence, insupportable, oppressive.

Betty horribly wanted Tommy; it seemed that she had never wanted anything else, so the slow hours had stretched.

Between two and three the city shook with a stronger motion, more violent and prolonged. In the streets buildings must surely be falling.... Betty went out to see.

Others, too, had gone out, fleeing from the danger of roofs and walls, or merely seeking companionship in blind fear. The streets were thronged; the churches were full of praying and crying. The *carabinieri* and the *guardie municipali* kept order as best they could among a crowd on the verge of hysteria. Here and there trooped in file homeless peasants from the ruined villages, their possessions bound on their backs or the backs of their beasts. From the comments tossed about one might infer this disaster to be probably the work of the good God or of the Evil One, or merely the spontaneous freakish rage of the eternally cursed mountain. Each view had its adherents.

Betty, at a street corner, ran into Luli. Like all the others, he was a shadow to her, a shadow to whom she said:

'Have you seen Tommy?'

He had not seen Tommy; he walked with her, helping her to look for Tommy; he was to her a shadow moving at her side, who spoke and was answered nothing. His speaking was:

'How should we find him to-night? It's hopeless. He'll turn up all right in the morning; there's nothing to be frightened about.'

It was irrelevant; Betty heard it as from a great distance; she was looking for Tommy—looking for him at street corners, going up steep climbing *vicoli* and down again, searching all the faces in the crowd. The shadow kept patiently at her side, with a shrug for the folly of it. The storm and the earthquake had certainly dazed her, set her wits wandering; he advised her many times to go home and sleep, since the shocks were now over and would very likely not recur.

'Tommy may be home by now,' the shadow said.

Betty shook her head; she knew that in the dim room nothing stirred but the flickering lamp. She looked for Tommy.

Out of the Toledo they came into the Piazza del Plebiscito, and so down the Strada del Gigante to Santa Lucia by the sea, where Tommy was so often, but was not now. Looking from Santa Lucia across the black bay, they saw the blazing game that the fiery cone was still playing untired; the earth's groaning sounded above the sweeping of the shaken sea.

Into the town they plunged again, Betty and the protesting shadow, who wanted to go to bed. The storm had dropped; upon the wind of dawn came the red rain of the cinders, the black clouds of the dust, blinding and choking. Behind these the grey morning grew; a dim day broke slowly on the tired, shaken city.

Since he could not prevail on Betty to go home, Luli went home himself; he could not walk the streets all night looking for Tommy, who was, no doubt, well amused somewhere.

'It isn't a fit night for you to be out,' he told Betty, 'but I am falling asleep: I must have rest. What would you have? You'd much better go home too.'

So they parted.

Betty took to going into all the churches she came to, to see if Tommy was there. She would sit down by the door and look at the praying people—the churches were thronged to-night—and dreamily wander into hazy speculations, soothed by the chanting voices and the sweet, heavy air, till she woke with a start, and so out again into the dim city, where the ashes came riding on the east wind like rain.

Once a *carabiniere* asked her where she was going, why she walked alone so in the disturbed city. She said:

'I am looking for my brother. Have you seen him? He is like me, only he carries a sketch-book and a pencil; and what do you suppose is likely to have happened to him?'

The *carabiniere* conveyed by a shrug that he could not say.

'But something is more likely to happen to you. It's a bad night to be walking in the town. All kinds of ruffians are about.'

That, being irrelevant, Betty did not hear.

It was strange how every one was abroad in Naples to-night. In the Piazza Sant' Angelo, a little after five o'clock, Betty met Warren Venables. She said to him:

'Help me, please, to find Tommy.'

He looked gently at her—they had hurt one another so badly that nothing but gentleness seemed possible between them now—and divined (it was a fresh hurt to him) how entirely he was a shadow to her; how the world was a crowded shadow-land, through which she moved alone, seeking the one reality, her other self. His discernment let him realize how all things but one must have slipped away through the wild hours of the night. He knew it by her wide, unseeing eyes, her strained, sallow face, the mechanic words, which were her only greeting. He was glad to be able to do her at least this service; he was glad to be at her side, taking care of her, though it might be only as an unnoticed shadow. It was in his mind, but not in hers, how she had not long since begged him not to see her any more.

He said gently:

'You're tired; you must go home. Tommy is all right.'

She said:

'I want Tommy. Help me, please, to find Tommy.'

He walked at her side, through the rain of the dust, which lay thick on the streets and gritted underfoot as they walked. Neither ever forgot that harsh gritting, or the sulphurous breath of that dim dawn. It hurt them both in memory for always.

There is a narrow alley which leads up out of the Strada San Biagio, climbing a little. They went up it—Betty neglected no street—and there they found Tommy.

Some scaffolding had fallen, tossed down by the storm or the earthquake, in a corner where no one passed. Tommy lay with his face to the street, his sketch-book clutched in the hand of one flung-out arm, the other arm pinned to his side, with a twelve-foot plank across his back and two poles across his legs. Tommy and the scaffolding both wore a coat an inch deep of black dust.

Venables lifted away the plank: it took most of his strength; then he moved the poles. Then he turned Tommy over very gently, and the black dust drifted down on to the upturned face. Betty raised it on to her lap and shielded it with her two hands, saying always, and not knowing what she said:

'Tommy—Tommy—Tommy.'

Venables said:

'I will fetch help. I will be as quick as I can.'

She looked at him with unseeing eyes. He paused a moment, then turned and left her, slipping away into the shadows, one of a world of shadows, leaving those two alone together, as, for her, they had been alone together through all the long night.

She looked down into her lap, and made a shield of her two hands, and muttered:

'Tommy—Tommy.'

CHAPTER XI
THE ETERNAL ROADS

> 'We are the creatures of birth, of ancestry, of circumstance; we are surrounded by law, physical and psychical.... The ways are dark, and the grey years bring a mysterious future which we cannot see.'—J. H. Shorthouse.

> 'The law of the past cannot be eluded, The law of the present and future cannot be eluded, The law of the living cannot be eluded—it is eternal.'—Walt Whitman.

There was peace in Naples, and sunshine breaking at last through clouds—rest and brightness following days of fear. It remained to put things together—all the broken things, human and otherwise. The city was full of those who reached hopeless hands for prop and support, having lost everything; full of those who gathered closely to them the fragments that remained, fragments they had snatched from ruin and clutched in their arms as they fled.

On the many dead, the many broken and dying, the many who grasped fragments, the many who had lost all, the clear sun looked down, on this 13th of April, with its gay, lucid light. It seemed to hold a promise, to mention a hope far off. It seemed to drag the world out of the dark pit, to give the task of rehabilitation and reconstruction the air, not of a far dream, but of a possibility—far too. It gave it also the air, quite definitely, of a necessity. It was like the first youth of the spring, with its forgetting of the black storms past, its promise of a brave renewal.

Betty Crevequer walked home through the sunny streets from the hospital. The gay sun had lit the long ward, sending dusty beams across the room to the broken, bandaged figures in the beds. By the side of one of the broken, bandaged figures Betty had sat and talked, and Tommy had talked too, to-day for the first time—talked for the first time, that is, in the Crevequers' generous sense of that elastic word.

Betty had for four days known that Tommy would not die, but live; now the sunshine in the streets brought her to a more vivid realization of it.

The sunshine in the streets, the keen smell of the sea that caught her breath as she turned down towards it, the fresh wind from the west, blowing the ashes away from Naples, brought sudden tears to her eyes, sudden, vague thoughts of far-off renewals, of the mending of all broken things. In her weariness she could not stay the tears; they stood in her eyes and quivered to her lashes. When she had climbed up to the little room at the top of the steep stairs, they took her wholly; she leaned her chin on her two hands and looked out over the city, not knowing whether the tears dropping slowly were for the old things broken and spilt, or for the slow mending that might yet be. Anyhow, the city lying so in the afternoon sunshine had a most sad gaiety. It brought back to Betty how Tommy's smile had to-day flickered out from the bandages, lightening the sad eyes.

She was horribly tired; it seemed that she had been living at high pressure, not only for these past few days—she could not count them—but for days and weeks before that. The time comes when strung nerves break like worn-out fiddle-strings; there is no more strength in them.

So, in her hour of weakness, Betty wept, having fallen through the broken floor of circumstance till she touched bottom, looking without hope at some far, possible ascent, through the sad dimness of tears. The west wind dried her tears on her face as she looked out; and Prudence Varley came in.

Betty turned and faced her, as she paused for a moment to knock at the open door, standing with chin a little raised to suit with the caught-up lip, straight and tall, with the grey, artist's eyes that took in everything and had been wont to give out nothing. Betty's mournful eyes met the look with her new, sad comprehension of that restraint which had always so held back everything. Yet now it seemed that it did not so entirely hold back everything; its remoteness was less complete. Betty hardly knew this; she knew chiefly how the room was tawdry and breathed of stale smoke, how the table was littered with cards and *Marchese Peppino*, how the other had come, perhaps, straight from a cool place, smelling cleanly of paint, full of the April sunshine, spacious and pure and bare.

Prudence Varley said:

'How do you do? May I come in? or——'

She paused, waiting. Betty was hardly used to such waiting on the part of her visitors; as a rule they came in, deeming questions superfluous.

Betty considered it for a moment, her lower lip caught between her teeth, her eyes pondering. She might, she knew, have said 'No.' Prudence

Varley neither offered nor demanded adornment of speech. It was an open question she had asked, to be answered truly. 'No' would have sent her simply away without comment or offence.

Betty considered 'No,' and rejected it, perhaps because the direct eyes seemed no longer to hold everything back; perhaps because, like a child hurt and bewildered, she wanted help; perhaps because, from the first to the last, she had always so liked Prudence Varley.

She said 'Yes,' and came forward and cleared a space in her own chair, and sat down herself on the arm of Tommy's. The clearing of Tommy's would have been too arduous a task.

Prudence sat down simply, unembarrassed. But Betty's thin, childish fingers, clasped round her knee, worked nervously in and out; she clenched her teeth over her lower lip.

'How is your brother?' Prudence said.

'B-better. He talked to-day, quite a lot.'

That extremely probable fact, Prudence perhaps thought, could hardly be taken as conclusive proof of the Crevequers' good health. But she said:

'I am very glad. Then he may be up before very long, perhaps?'

'I don't know how long; they c-can't tell me.' Betty stammered a good deal over it. She paused for recovery. 'When he's well enough,' she resumed, 'we want to go north for a rest.'

'To England?'

'No. Oh no; that w-wouldn't be a rest. To Santa Caterina. It's our home; we used to live there.... Tommy won't be able to do much for some time.'

'No; of course. You won't come back till the autumn, when it's cooler, I expect.'

The two looks met, the one faintly questioning and half asking pardon for the question, the other with all its depth of sad bewilderment stirred—a miserable gaze like a child's.

'I don't know,' said Betty, and bit her lip. Then quite suddenly the depths surged up and broke through. Her sad eyes hung on the lucid grey ones that looked with such gentleness at her. 'I don't know—oh, I don't know.... I don't know what we can do ... how we're to do it.... Can't you tell me?... Because it's been you, you know, who've spoilt things.... And what next?'

Prudence accepted it, meeting the claim with puckered brows of thought. She did not know what next. She was an idealist, of a continual and never-failing hope; but, striving to see, she saw only roads running eternally sundered, as Betty too had seen them from the first hour of comprehension.

Betty said again, half to herself, how they were spoilt, the old things. 'And what new things can there be, ever, for us?' On Prudence, who had done her share of the spoiling, she still made her stammering claim, blind-eyed, without hope.

Prudence's response to it was a doubting question.

'If they're spoilt then ... you'll leave them?'

Betty's eyes hung on hers.

'You mean not come back here? Oh, we don't want to; I've told you that's spoilt. But where else?... Tommy couldn't get anything to do at Santa Caterina.'

Prudence said there were other places in Italy for a journalist. Or perhaps even England.... But at that Betty shook her head. No spoilt things should drive her to that place of damp half-lights.

'Not England. We couldn't live there; it's never, never warm.... Perhaps Genoa; we know it so well. But Tommy may not find anything to do; he's never been on a regular, proper paper....' Swiftly, at *Marchese Peppino*, the colour surged over her face; the room was so full of it. She said quickly, a sudden throbbing of helpless anger choking her speech: 'That, too—that, too—everything—you've spoilt it—and w-what can you give us instead?'

'What would you take?' Prudence said, with a very grave and very gentle directness, turning the tables thus.

Betty's sad regard, emptied of anger, owned them turned. But she felt a sudden desire to know.

'If we could take anything ... would you give it? You?'

The emphasis on the pronoun put it in the singular number, thus setting Betty's own acceptance or refusal of offerings outside the range of question and answer, as she had meant. For she was very tired of talking about that. To the personal question Prudence, after a full minute of thinking it over, returned a deliberating answer:

'I don't quite know.'

It was indeed what she had been for some time wondering. But the spoken words seemed to strike her with a sense of incompleteness, of a gap somewhere between themselves and the thought they should have accurately fitted. Prudence, who did not very often clothe her thoughts, was fastidious, when she did, about the garments' fit. She tried something else—a dubious 'I can't be sure, but I suppose ... in the end ... I probably should.'

Betty watched the doubtful pondering. She said:

'You mean because you would think we had a claim? Yes, I know.'

And Prudence returned slowly:

'A little that. But that shouldn't count much.... There would be other things, and they would all have to be weighed.... It wouldn't be easy.'

'No,' Betty said; 'I suppose not. So it's just as well, really, that it can't come to that, that we can't take anything—not either of us, not ever, because of all the things between.'

Then, all the things between growing with the words to insistence, Betty mentioned some of them, impelled, now the barriers were so breaking, to have everything clear.

'There are so many things.... There's all the money we owe. We must pay it back.'

Prudence silently assented. She wondered how much the Crevequers owed Warren Venables.

'There are c-crowds of other things,' the sad voice stammered on—'everything, almost.... But you know it all. You have known it all the time.'

Their eyes met and looked away. Prudence did not at all deny that she had known it all the time.

'You've all of you known it all the time,' went on the dreary voice, without anger, without hope. Anger had been spent before, on another of those who had 'known it all the time.' (The passionate fires of the days of reparation had burned resentment to ashes, and on these had dropped the tears of pity and pain.) Hope there was none. 'But Tommy and I—we've only got to know it lately, you see. We—we didn't understand before. But we understand now. We understand why—why you wouldn't be friends with us.'

Prudence looked away sadly. It was terrible to have to accept it all so, denying nothing. She wanted to heal, but knew no way.

In the pause Betty took up a cigarette-case from Tommy's chair, mechanically fingering it. Then abruptly she dropped it, and looked defiantly up.

'But lots of people do that—the other sort—your sort!' she cried.

Imagination, in these days so morbidly alive, continually invented for her attacks unthought of, and called out defence to meet what needed none. For discrimination was of so new a growth.

Prudence said quickly, 'But I know—oh, I know! Please don't!'— protesting, apologizing for the existence of this gulf, which had so yawned to exaggeration. Such an over-recognition of it as that last had implied hurt her more than what had gone before; it showed so vividly how the Crevequers staggered under their new knowledge, pitifully unsteady as yet on the fresh ground. She said presently, having thought things over: 'If I have been horrid, and hurt you, I beg your pardon. I am very sorry.'

'It's just you,' said Betty, 'out of all of you, you know, who oughtn't to say that. Because you pretended nothing. You kept everything back, all along, instead of—instead of giving everything but just one thing—oh, well.' She could not speak of that. She ended with half a laugh. 'Nobody, you know, could have thought for a moment that you liked us.'

'I suppose not,' said Prudence simply. She went on, with something between explanation and apology: 'You see, I'm not like Aunt Ida; I don't write.' Betty was grateful to her for making the comparison solely with her Aunt Ida. 'People to me are simply people....'

Betty nodded.

'I know. Not—not copy.'

'And, you see, friendship isn't a name to me. It's something rather real and serious. I make friends slowly, I suppose.'

'And you didn't want to make friends with us. Oh, I know.'

'As I saw it, it wouldn't have been fair, you see,' Prudence explained very gently, looking away, asking forgiveness with her voice.

Betty assented.

'No; it wouldn't have been very fair.'

So their past intercourse was defined in few words. That done, Prudence turned to the present.

'But now—now it would be fair—if you will.'

Betty shook her head. Prudence had supposed that she would.

'No, not now. That wouldn't at all do.'

They rested on that for a minute before Betty went on.

'Tommy and I have got each other; and that is the way it must be, the way we've got to do it—don't you see?'

Her eyes seemed to entreat Prudence to see, to make, if she could, others see.

'It's like this,' the sad tones stammeringly explained. 'We're in a mess, Tommy and I; and we've got to get out of it somehow, if we can—find, you know, things we don't hate, things to go on with. That's all we want: to go on somehow and be happy, as we used to be happy. You know, you can't be happy if you're wishing all the time to have things you can't have, and to be things you can't be. So, either we must stop wishing—and we may do that in time—or we must find new things that we like. But that's bound to be a long job.' No movement of Prudence's demurred to that; its truth stared one in the face. 'And perhaps we can't do that; perhaps things stick always.'

And to that, too, no denial came from the idealist of continual hope, who yet saw the eternal roads running.

Betty, because she, too, saw their running, said finally:

'I suppose, really, one stays pretty much the same sort of person to the end.... And that's all right, as long as one doesn't run up against other sorts; it hurts to do that'—at the pain of that clash of codes her brows knit—'and that's why we won't try m-mixing the sorts; it wouldn't be what you call fair, on either sort.'

Prudence heard the finality in that: it found its echo in her soul; but still she pleaded Warren's cause (he cared so much) with:

'But if both cared to.... Oh, that isn't quite all there is to it, I know—I'm not a fool who can only see one thing—but it's a thing that should count a great deal. Of all the many, many things, I believe that's the one that, perhaps, in the end counts most.'

Betty admitted it.

'More than any one other; but not more than all the others together. You see, there are rather many, and it wouldn't do. It wouldn't w-work, you know it wouldn't; and—and it would hurt rather.... Oh, it wouldn't do.'

She clenched her lip again between her teeth, perhaps to steady it.

Prudence thought it all over, admitting it true, before saying, with a quick tremor in her own voice:

'But, perhaps, sometime—afterwards....'

Betty unclasped her hands from her knee and leaned her chin on them, and looked straight in front of her.

'No,' she said; 'I think never. Then she gave it a turn, swerving as usual from her own part, with 'You know it—you yourself.'

Prudence said nothing. That she knew it hardly needed affirmation; she knew it with such a sad, hopeless certainty. For the eternal roads run straitly, and their running is between gateless walls. The grey, artist's eyes were suddenly wet and blind, with a swift surging of many feelings. Seeing them, Betty said again:

'It wouldn't work—for any of us,' with a new gentle cadence in her tone. Then she went on: 'Tommy and I have got each other. We can help each other, and no one else in the world can help us. Don't you see? Because we know each other so awfully well; we mean a good deal to each other, you know. There's always been just us two. There always will be, and that's the one thing that really matters—the one thing that always will matter. In the end no one else c-counts.'

In that was the ring of certainty; it had not needed to be thought out; it was as if it had always been there, waiting to be defined.

After a moment Betty went on, with this time a little tremor in the tired monotony of her voice.

'I think I should like you to understand—how it's been, you know, always. We've had each other, but we've had no one else much, ever. We rather brought ourselves up; we weren't taught anything about—well, all the things that I suppose you were taught. We came to England when we were about thirteen and fourteen; we hated it, the awful w-weather and all our relations. Directly Tommy left school we came back to Italy, and—well, Tommy got work here. And we knew nobody but—but—well, you probably know the sort our friends are; I expect the others have told you,' she added in parenthesis, with a passing glint of laughter, remembering how Prudence had not sought the close acquaintance which should enable her to know. 'We're very fond of them,' she added, and affection submerged the laughter; 'we've had g-good times together. Well, we hadn't much to live on, and the people round us gambled and ran up debts, and never paid them till they had to; and we did, too. We didn't think—or care—whether the things we did were decent, or honest, or anything of that sort. We just went on from day to day, playing round with each other and our friends, and we were very happy.... I don't think, somehow, that we've ever had a proper chance.... And when you j-judge us, you might, perhaps, remember that.'

Prudence, who had listened gravely in silence, as always, said now:

'How should I judge you, or you me? I have not done that, ever.'

Betty said, smiling a little sadly:

'No; you only—you only kept away. I know.... But all the same, I should like you to understand a little.'

'I do understand,' said Prudence.

'Well, when we met all of you last winter, we didn't know the difference—or didn't care, anyhow. We thought it was funny; and it was, rather—Mrs. Venables, you know, and being s-studied, and—and all that——' Laughter flickered again to the sad eyes, but died swiftly. 'And then, after some time, we got to understand.' The stammering monotone was expressionless and hard. 'And ... well, that's all.... We've both of us rather minded.... I have been angry, I suppose, about some things; but that's all done now.... And now we've kind of come to see that the old things are no good any more—all spoilt, anyhow for now—and we've got to go and look for new things, and perhaps we shan't find them; but anyhow no one else can help.'

'I am sorry,' said Prudence Varley, after a moment, being able to offer, it seemed, no help but that. Her eyes asked forgiveness, because, having helped to break, she could have no share in the mending. She knew it was true that 'we can help each other, and no one else in the world can help us.'

To her sorrow, Betty returned, 'We've got each other, you know,' and even smiled a little. They had so nearly lost that possession.

Prudence got up, and stood close to the small figure on the chair-arm, her hands clasped behind her. She was not demonstrative; where some people might kiss, she merely stood and spoke.

'You've thought, I dare say,' she said gently, 'that I've been standing on a pedestal and looking down—a horrid prig. Well, I suppose I have been a prig; I am made so, and I am sorry. But—please believe this—I haven't been on a pedestal; I've only been shut in between walls. Oh, you know as well as I do that we each have walls all round us, and it's not easy to knock them down; they shut us in.... But sometimes gaps come in them, so that we can see through—see the landscape outside, and all the other roads running. I suppose, perhaps, there have come lately gaps in all our walls. Anyhow, I should like to thank you for the gaps in mine. I hope very much they will not get bricked up again.... Being shut into dark, narrow paths prevents one from seeing anything outside—the daylight and all the other roads. But of course when a gap is made, one looks out through it. And looking out means looking up.' She paused a moment, and added softly, looking over the dark head out of the window: 'I think, you know, we're all trying to make what amends we can by looking up now, if we ever looked at all down. I hope you entirely believe that; and I hope you'll remember it, and not too much hate us, when you think about us at all.'

The silence that followed was broken by a sudden sob. The dark head was bowed; Betty broke down utterly into crying for the second time that day. Her tears shook her; she could say no word.

A hand was on the bowed shoulder.

'Don't—oh, don't'

The sobs died at last chokingly away to long, shaken breaths.

'Please go now,' said Betty. 'Thank you for—for everything, and for saying that just now. And I don't know why I cried—only I'm so t-tired. And you can't do anything more. And please go now, if you don't mind.'

'I suppose,' said Prudence, 'it's good-bye. We're leaving Naples next week.... But sometime later we may meet again, all of us.... And meanwhile, if there's anything we can do—ever——'

'Only leave us your address, please. We'll send what we borrowed; we've not got it just now. And will you please say good-bye for us to—to Mrs. Venables and your cousins?'

'Keep them away,' the sad eyes entreated; and Prudence promised, 'Yes; I will.'

She stood for a moment longer by the small crouched figure with its bent, dark head; her eyes were full of her powerless, ineffectual desires to heal, to help. Having the gift of comprehension, she wholly knew their ineffectualness. She could only go, for all had been said between them, and there remained the doing, wherein she had no part nor lot.

She turned and went down into the city, and saw with wet eyes how it was full of the sunshine, with the sea-wind blowing through it like hope.

CHAPTER XII
THE ROADS DIVIDE

> 'So much fate, so much irresistible dictation from temperament and unknown inspiration, enters into life, that we doubt we can say anything out of our own experience whereby to help each other.'—R. W. Emerson.

Prudence, according to her promise, exerted herself to keep her family from going to say good-bye to the Crevequers. It was not a very easy task. She represented to her aunt that looking after Tommy took most of Betty's time.

'I doubt if they allow her at the hospital much,' said Mrs. Venables; 'and the child must be terribly anxious and lonely. I should like to do what I can for her.'

Mrs. Venables was very kind; late failures of intimacy had slipped from her memory since Tommy's disaster. She had been to see him at the hospital, and had met Betty there. Tommy, during her visit, had apparently been asleep. Betty had hardly spoken, for fear, she said, of waking him.

'It is a long time,' said Mrs. Venables, 'since I had a satisfactory talk with either of those interesting children. Yes, Prudence, they *are* interesting, owing to their very peculiar circumstances and ways of life, whatever may be their personal limitations. I grant that one does not come across great depths in them—or, anyhow, that the depths are as yet quite unstirred; but those childlike, seemingly almost soulless natures are a most interesting study to me. One wonders how far their climate and their faith contribute towards the result as we see it. There is certainly something in the beauty and gay paganism of this city, mingled as it is with the simple devoutness of a symbolic faith, that seems to develop such characters freely. I should like to watch those children's career—to see what they grow into. Who knows but that they may sometime find their souls? That would be a strange consummation, deeply impressive; I should much like to try to bring it about, but I am afraid the time is very far from ripe as yet. However, I should at all events wish to see them once again before we part. We have, after all, attained to some intimacy, they and I; we have shared so many vivid experiences, and had so much striking talk together.'

But Mrs. Venables was at last induced to put her parting words into a letter—four sheets, closely written. Betty took it to read to Tommy, and they composed an answer together, with immense pains, resisting manfully the temptations to 'strike' which assailed them.

'And so that's the end of Mrs. Venables,' said Betty, sighing as she signed her name. 'And I suppose no one will ever think us so interesting again.... I wonder, Tommy, if we made the most of our opportunities....'

They mournfully pondered over the unreturning past. Yet they had certainly made, if not the most, at any rate a good deal, of those regretted opportunities. They had, both purposely and accidentally, succeeded in being a real and profound impression. When they arrived at the age that in their opinion justified them in reading Mrs. Venables' works, they would probably get much pleasure out of their own portraits.

Miranda Venables came to see Betty the day before her family left Naples. She came in with a dejected air.

'I've come to say good-bye. We're going to-morrow. It'll be rather ripping getting home and getting some cricket and tennis, only I'm simply too awfully slack for anything after all this fooling round doing nothing. Feel.' She held out a plump arm for Betty to pinch. 'Horrid flabby, isn't it? And I say, I'm awfully sick at having to say good-bye, you know.'

The round face was tragically despondent. Miranda had scarcely realized till now how much she liked the Crevequers. She said so.

'You are rotters, you two, but you do make things go, you know,' she explained, a little embarrassed at her own frankness. 'And, I say, I hope we all meet again sometime—not in this beastly place, but at home. You might come and stay with us; you'd get some hockey. Oh, I forgot; you don't care about doing things. But it's beastly saying good-bye. I hate it.'

'So do I,' Betty said. 'So I never do it. Let's not. Let's come and have ices instead.'

They went and had ices at Caflisch's, and the pathos of the occasion was salient. Miranda, after the second ice, worked up at length to:

'It's all very well, but I like your sort of people, if it *is* different (like Warren said once, and mother says), a jolly sight better than ours—so there!'

'It's all a q-question of taste, of course,' Betty said. 'And now I must go; and as we aren't going to say good-bye, there's no more to be said. I hope we shall all of us have a j-jolly summer.'

'Please say good-bye for me,' said Miranda tearfully, referring to Tommy, who had a pedestal of his own. 'And I hope he'll soon be better, and … oh dear!'

So that parting was effected. It should, after all, count for something that one's friends should weep to say good-bye.

Next day the Venables left Naples.

When she knew that they had gone, Betty seemed to lose suddenly the strength she had summoned to her for resistance; she had no more need of it; the long struggle was over. She shivered a little at that past bitterness, and buried her face in her two hands. When she looked up again, the past lay, as it were, slain; all the future waited.

The struggle, made so hard and bitter at the first, had at the last been easy. Warren Venables had let it rest in the end, realizing bitterly at last the ineffectualness of contest. Prudence had assisted him to that realization.

'We can't do anything for them now; we're no good to them; we only hurt them. We've got to leave them alone.'

It was strange to Warren to see how her eyes were wet.

'It's easy enough for you,' he said, his voice hard and level. 'You don't know how much I care.'

She said, very gently, 'I do,' and then was silent for a moment, thinking perhaps that what she did not know was rather how much she herself might possibly have cared, had many things been wholly different; had not the unconquerable 'there is nothing to say' finally summed up the situation as far as her part in it went. But of those vague might-have-beens Warren knew nothing.

Prudence said:

'I do know. And that's why you'll leave them alone—because you care. For if you don't, you'll hurt them—horribly. Don't you see? We've hurt them enough; this is the only amends possible—the only amends they will take.'

'Amends!' His face was set like a flint, his way when he was hurt. 'That's just it. I've been a brute all along; and when I came to know it, through *their* coming to know it, and through my coming to care so much, I wasn't allowed to make any amends. That's what I can't stand.'

(He had been shaken and stirred of late out of all his self-containment; Prudence had heard many things from him.)

'You've made your amends,' she said. 'First by the things you've said to her; and now you will be making them again by leaving her alone, as she wishes. There's no other you can make. Don't you see?'

'I see I've got to,' he said harshly. 'I've been made to see that clearly enough lately. Oh, I suppose I've got to accept it—sit down under it.'

Prudence mused over it.

'It's been rather strange all along,' she said, more to herself than to him. 'For we did our part to them, for good or evil, and they theirs to us, by accident, and now that it's done we can't be of any more use to each other, in the straits we're all, I suppose, in, through all we've come to see and know. They want nothing of us, and we had better want nothing of them; our uses for each other are over; there it is, you see. They must leave us to help ourselves, and we must leave them to help themselves and each other. And I hope we shall all do that; only it will have to be along our own lines, not along other people's. You can't step out of your own road into somebody else's; there are chasms between, too wide to jump. And if you do manage to jump them, you don't know the geography of the new road, and you only lose your way. I can't help being stiff and puritanical and disliking certain things. They can't help being—well, street-children of gregarious habits and wide tastes. Why should they? It's merely being themselves. But though I may be a prig, I can yet try to understand and not to keep aloof; and though they may be—well, they can improve their roads too. It's always open to us to improve our own roads—only not, I think, successfully to leave them.'

Thus Prudence, working it out for her own satisfaction, her considering brows puckered over the light that her thought had kindled in her farseeing, discerning artist's eyes. This side of it—the moral side, the ultimate side, call it what you will—was of salient clearness to her; it predominated, rising vividly out of the tangle of issues. It was to her the thing that greatly mattered, that it was always open to us to improve our own roads.

To Warren (the discrimination was partly, perhaps, one of sex, a good deal between the idealist and one who was not, whatever he was, at all an idealist) what may be called the moral aspect was obscured. He had wanted something and had failed to get it; that for him summed up the matter. Later, he might come to realize many things, all the things that Prudence realized, that the Crevequers realized—how the fusion of two 'sorts' was at the best a rash experiment, at the worst a most tragic catastrophe; how the matter had been, no doubt, wisely decided. Now he knew but one thing: what he so greatly desired he might not have. Prudence's vision of it seemed of little relevance to him. They might all follow their improved roads anywhere they chose; they might climb heights, in that grey future wherein he at least must be (so it seemed to him at this time) a solitary pedestrian; how they might help themselves and each other concerned him not at all.

His clever face was very bitterly set as he stared at the ground, brooding over it. It was probable that he too had learned something, the insolence, as his cousin had termed it, of his past attitude having so recoiled upon himself.

'Oh,' said Prudence, suddenly, following up her own talk of roads, 'I wish we *could* leave them—I wish we could; but walls shut us in. The walls of character, and circumstances, and old habit; we can't break through them. We only knock against them—and it hurts.' She stopped, because her voice shook strangely. After a moment she said quietly: 'We can't do that. We can only try to keep the gaps wide, and look through them…. But there are one or two things we can do besides that. Mr. Crevequer will want to get something to do afterwards; I told you, didn't I, that they are giving everything up.'

'Oh! That charming paper. About time, too, I should say. Well?'

'Well, I thought you might write to that *Settimana Illustrata* man you know at Genoa. They are going to their old home for the present; but eventually they would like work at Genoa. I should think the *Settimana* might give him something to start on; he's quite clever, of course; and he really can draw, can't he? Genoa's near their home. They'll have all their old friends to play with, and of course they'll make new ones, and of course their friends will be of all sorts; their road takes them there. What I don't know,' she added presently, 'is where else it is going to take them, and where ours are going to take us.'

Warren did not think it particularly mattered, and said so. Prudence, who did, proceeded to explain to herself, rather than to him, where their roads had, in the past, taken them. She liked to be quite sure, to arrive at sureness by thinking things thoroughly out.

'We've all been wrong, and all through different lacks in us—different failures of understanding. I've hated ugliness so much that I haven't tried—I haven't even wanted—to see the beauty that's always tangled into it. I've just looked the other way. That was through being a prig, and stupid. You've minded ugliness so little (though you've seen it all right) that you've accepted it, traded on it. That was through being lacking in some sense—I think, perhaps, the sense of beauty, and a little in the moral sense, too.' Prudence was being offensively frank, as she was apt to be when she thought things out aloud. 'And the Crevequers haven't known, really, what ugliness was. That was through never having learnt, chiefly. And,' she summed up after a moment, 'there we all stand.'

'So it seems,' Warren said. 'It must be a satisfaction to have it all so clearly arranged.'

Prudence went on, undisturbed.

'And what I should like to know is where we shall eventually stand. You say it doesn't matter; of course, as a matter of fact, it is the one thing which does. Where we go, and what we see by the way—oh, what else is there?'

'Where we mayn't go,' Warren answered her drearily, 'and what we miss by the way. It matters more, for it's better—more worth going to, better worth seeing.'

To that she said nothing. They both thought of it all, silently: of how four ways had come together for a little at the cross roads, how those who travelled along them had met and spoken and taken again the parted ways, where they ran beyond range of sight into a grey land, towards horizons blind with mist—blind and dark to one of the two who stood now and looked; but to the other limitless, luminous, soft with the shrouded brightness of the dawn.

'Oh,' said Prudence presently, her thought running on what we miss by the way, 'we—our sort of people—being so respectable and so honest and so refined, sit on our pedestals and look down and talk and analyse, because we've got a few things that they haven't; but, really, I am looking up all the time. For, whatever they haven't got and haven't done, they've at all events lived. They keep on doing that all the time; they always will, in whatever particular way they do it. It's such an immense thing, that. Living is like an art, that some people never learn at all; I suppose the Crevequers were born knowing it—they had no need to learn it. And if they haven't learnt quite all about it yet, well, that's only a question of time. They've got the genius of it all right. That's what I look up to in them. And,' she added, since the Crevequers were being so thoroughly thought out, 'they have another thing—the best thing they've got, the thing that will in the end matter, however much everything else fails—they have each other.'

At that Warren's face took a greater bitterness.

'So I was given to understand,' he said. 'I was told that they, being so much the same sort, wanted no other companionship. The combination of either with anyone else, it seemed, would not work—would be a disastrous fiasco, in fact.'

Prudence acknowledged his right to his bitterness, the hurt being still so new and sore, his anger with himself going so deep.

But she said, after a moment, pleading, 'Don't grudge them that. For, do you see, it's about all they've got left,' and so ended, with wet eyes.

CHAPTER XIII
PINE-BARK BOATS

'I thenke forto touche also
The world which neweth every dai,
So as I can, so as I mai.'—John Gower.

'Earth loves her young: a preference manifest.'—George Meredith.

A dozen or so of the Crevequers' friends came down to the harbour to see them off to Santa Caterina. The Crevequers leaned over the rail of the crowded launch, which was bearing them out to the *König Albrecht,* and waved their hands and stammered good-bye to every one. Tommy was very weak and wan, and carried one arm in a sling; he had been out of hospital for just a week. That week they had spent in selling most of their effects, wringing out of their various debtors, with much exertion, some of the money owed them, and raising in the end quite a creditable sum, with which they paid their extensive debts and booked their passage by sea, and finally, having a little over, asked about a dozen of their most intimate friends to a supper-party at the Trattoria Pallino, on the Vomero. There, last night, they had said good-bye.

Last night had been full of regrets—the sadness of parting, the pathos of a merry company broken—a pathos hidden in jests, yet oppressive, nevertheless, in the blue May twilight. They had sat beneath the hanging purple veil of the wistaria, and the sweetness of the May roses had mingled with the blue fragrance of the Tuscan cigars to which Tommy had recklessly risen, and through the sweetness and the fragrance the salt keenness of the sea had pierced, and its washing edge had whispered a soft undertone to the city sounds that rang up through the still evening air. They had looked down and seen how the spreading city far below bloomed like a great rose of many colours in the soft falling twilight; how the sky and the sea were still delicately flushed with the afterglow; how, above the flattened cone of Vesuvius, a great yellow moon swung up into the blue still east. It had looked upon the city with a large, mellow charity, softly touching its many colours, deepening the steep shadows of the streets that ran through it like gorges. It had laid a broad yellow path for itself across the blue spaces of the evening sea, and so twilight had deepened tenderly to night.

They had all drunk to each other in red Posilipo, and wished themselves and each other good luck, and Gina Lunelli had said, for the twentieth time, 'You won't find any place so good to live in as Naples,' and Tommy had said, 'You must come and stay with us some time at Santa Caterina—all of you,' with a comprehensive sweep of his arm, generous with the large hospitality of red Posilipo. Betty had said how Genoa, too, was a gay place, with plenty doing, only the winds that blew down its streets in winter were certainly evil and bitter, and one had to wear all one's clothes at once. But Santa Caterina was different; Italy certainly held no such other place, and they must, of course, one day all come and see.

Thus they talked, and laughed, and sang songs, and looked away from the city which held in its deep shadows so much of their life. It would have been quite easy then to slip down among the shadows and the colours and take that life again, broken as it was, in time perhaps forgetting everything. New beginnings were so hard, the call of the old things so insistent. The old things that they had of late so hated, as spoilers of their lives, they knew that they would not always hate—if now they went down into the shadowed streets and took them again, striving to forget, in the end all but forgetting, this cleavage which so lay across life. For all cleavages may be bridged with time.

So, sick-hearted, the Crevequers had looked at the old ways which so clogged them, which would possibly (why not?) always clog them, clinging heavily like mire; and at the new ways which they were seeking wearily, with no heart, with 'too late' echoing in their souls like a knell.

But this May morning, blown by a light wind that set the blue sea dancing and would soon make them very ill, astir with the thronging of ships in the harbour, and the hooting of voyages begun, was full of unquenchable hopes and unvanquished youth and gay beginnings.

Some one on the launch was playing 'Addio, bella Napoli' on a mandolin; the Crevequers called again 'Good-bye,' and leaned over the rail and watched the sea-face of the city, crowned by Castel St. Elmo on the hill, growing smaller in the distance. So much of life lay there....

They left it there, gold and dross, in that crucible which had so transmuted it. Gold or dross, it seemed to matter little; it had melted from them, burning their hands.

They looked at it once more, saw it dwindle far away, then turned together to the wide, blue newness of the sea.

Betty had to make both the boats, because Tommy could not yet use his right hand. She made them out of the pieces of red bark which flaked off the pine-trunks and lay in heaps by the edge of the pool. Each boat was about six inches long and two inches wide, square about the stern and pointed in the bows, with a pine-needle mast and an envelope sail. To prevent bitterness and evil speaking, Tommy had his choice of them when they were finished. Then they were launched, and the Crevequers lay and watched them, knowing that not for a long time need they go across to the other side to welcome them to port. They made a slow voyage in the windless afternoon. There was never much wind up here, though it was up among the hills, because the pines stood close and thick about the water, shutting it in to a deep green gloom.

The Crevequers lay by the water, upon the slippery brown needles, and drank in the warm resinous fragrance. It was always pleasant to step from the winding stone path, where the afternoon sun lay hot, where mule-carts climbed up and jingled their bells lazily, into this deep green shadowed place, where in the water the images of the pines nearly met from side to side, leaving a little circle of blue between. It had always been a favourite place; the Crevequers had spent much of their youth here, sailing pine-bark boats from side to side, hanging head downwards over the water with jars to catch water-beetles, bathing, or dangling an ineffectual line for fish.

They had spent the morning paddling about the seashore and among the rocks in the white canoe, which leaked horribly. Now they had come up here to get dry.

It was note-worthy how these weeks in Santa Caterina had left their healing touch upon both. They had been weeks of playing in the warm sunshine (there is nowhere else such sunshine, so bright and yet so gentle), of renewals of many friendships, with laughter and embraces, of rest and healing after strain of mind and body. Recuperation had begun its slow work. Tommy looked less ill, Betty less nervous and weary; laughter flickered from eyes sad and pondering, but not now, as a rule, unhappy.

With broken ways behind them, new roads in front of them as yet untried, they seemed thus to be waiting a little, putting fragments together, finding, as it were, their foothold, or perhaps seeking it, as yet blindly. Prudence Varley's optimism would doubtless have averred that the finding was only a matter of time. The Crevequers averred nothing; it was not in them to analyse, as Prudence analysed and thought out. But deep in their pondering eyes lay unsolved questions—questions they did not consciously put to themselves; questions as to the happy road they so blindly sought—whether it ran through new places or through old; whether, if through new, it could be reached, seeing that temperament, which had at least as much moulded circumstance as circumstance had forced temperament, was probably in the end master of all the roads, insisting that every one remained, as Betty had said, pretty much the same sort of person as he began.

If one was so to remain, it would perhaps be wiser to seek no more. For the basis of these new desires was, after all, so irremediably shattered. What the Crevequers did not know was whether the desires had any independent standing. For they would never be self-tormentors; they would seek always, and have a considerable gift for finding, the happiest way; they understood, as Prudence had said, the art of living well enough for that. But where that quest would lead them it was not given to them, not given to anyone, to know.

So, among all the confusion and the chaos of things broken and problems unsolved, two facts alone stood out, stable and unquestioned, inevitably sure. One was the complete breakage of the basis of their new desires—its scattering into fragments, never, whatever else might come to pass, to be pieced together. That destruction they had accepted; it was too inevitable for rebellion. They had left that behind them; and time would heal the memory, as time heals all hurts.

The other thing that emerged unquestionably out of the chaos was how they were together; how they had been together through everything; how they were together now, sailing pine-bark boats and seeking fresh roads; how, along any roads they might chance to find, they would journey together, knowing themselves admirable travelling-companions, knowing that to be well amused on the road is three-parts of the journey's hope. As Betty had said, 'We can help each other, and no one else in the world can help us. Because we know each other so awfully well. Don't you see?'

Prudence had seen—seen, too, that it was the best thing they had—the thing that would in the end matter, however much everything else failed. She had seen the Crevequers cast up, as it were, out of fire, holding this gold to them, when all else—the old and the new things alike—had melted from their hands.

And to all their questioning life could give them as yet this answer alone. The other answers would work themselves out through the veiled years, slowly, painfully perhaps. It was, then, a triumphant thing to have one possession safe for all time—one thing that the inscrutable years, and failure and joy and tears, could not touch; one thing, in a world of uncertain values, that the flames of the crucible would not at all transmute. It was, in fine, an admirable thing that they had one another to sail boats with.

Tommy was throwing stones, with his left hand, after his boat, with intent to hasten it. In the long run, even taking into account undoubted occasional successes, experience goes to show that this is not really a very useful thing to do, even when the right hand is used. Tommy's boat presently was struck and capsized.

'All right,' Tommy observed. 'Yours isn't going to come in to shore by itself—you needn't think it. We'll have a bombardment.... Mine was a rotten boat.... If I couldn't make a better boat than that.... There, that's got it. Now they can race in upside down. C-come round and get them.'

The race in upside down was a leisurely process. The owners got bored at last, and decided to abandon the crafts, which remained bobbing together upside down, twin derelicts far from the shore.

Out of the shadowed green pine-gloom the Crevequers came up again on to the steep, climbing hill-path, whose stones were hot with the evening sunshine. The warm still air was sweet with the pines, salt with the breath of the sea below. From up here, looking down through the silver-grey screen of the olives, one saw all the little bay lying, golden with the sunset, the sea stretching level and limpid, blue as evening, between jutting points, the fishing-city, pink and yellow and white, curving round it, set close on the still, clear, tideless edge, that was as a lake's margin, lifted by no ripple, but having for waves a soft soundless sway to and fro.

The Crevequers loved this waveless evening sea. Betty gave a little sigh of content, and slipped her hand into Tommy's.

'Come on,' she said, 'l-let's run down, and get r-really hot, then we'll go and upset ourselves out of the canoe. What fun.'

They did so.